"You kiss me as if you care."

"As if?" Rebecca smiled. "How else would I kiss you?"

Nick breathed a long sigh and gathered her against his chest. "Some people demand... some seduce...some manipulate. I am steeled against everything but the power of your tenderness."

His arms tightened around her for a moment, and she felt a surge of emotion pass through him. Then he abruptly let her go.

She searched his face. "Are you going to take it all back now? All the wonderful things...?"

"No," he answered flatly. "But you are so young. What do you know about love?"

She looked him squarely in the eye. "Who are you trying to protect? Me? Or you?"

The look in his eyes was sad. "Both of us."

WELCOME
TO THE WONDERFUL WORLD
OF *Harlequin Romances*

Interesting, informative and entertaining,
each Harlequin Romance portrays an appealing
and original love story. With a varied array
of settings, we may lure you on an African safari,
to a quaint Welsh village, or an exotic Riviera
location—anywhere and everywhere that adventurous
men and women fall in love.

As publishers of Harlequin Romances, we're
extremely proud of our books. Since 1949,
Harlequin Enterprises has built its publishing
reputation on the solid base of quality and
originality. Our stories are the most popular
paperback romances sold in North America; every
month, six new titles are released and sold at
nearly every book-selling store in Canada and the
United States.

For a list of all titles currently available,
send your name and address to:

HARLEQUIN READER SERVICE,
(In the U.S.) P.O. Box 52040, Phoenix, AZ 85072-2040
(In Canada) P.O. Box 2800, Postal Station A
5170 Yonge Street, Willowdale, Ont. M2N 6J3

We sincerely hope you enjoy reading
this Harlequin Romance.

Yours truly,

THE PUBLISHERS
Harlequin Romances

A Tender Season

Sarah Keene

Harlequin Books

TORONTO • NEW YORK • LONDON
AMSTERDAM • PARIS • SYDNEY • HAMBURG
STOCKHOLM • ATHENS • TOKYO • MILAN

ISBN 0-373-02698-6

Harlequin Romance first edition June 1985

CHAPTER ONE

STAGE FRIGHT. She had known the feeling before.... A few butterflies in the stomach on opening night of a college theater production, a dry throat and a light head before her commencement address. But nothing in her memory compared with this wave of white panic now rising from somewhere deep within.

Rebecca Yates glanced down at her small white-knuckled hands, frozen to the steering wheel of her rickety VW, and uttered a shaky little laugh. "I'm in great shape," she murmured to herself as she waited for the light to change. "By the time I get there, I'll be lucky if I can remember my own name." Taking a deep breath, she unclenched one clammy set of fingers and flexed them tremulously before her face.

The truth was, her excitement had been mounting steadily for the past two weeks. Ever since that afternoon Noel Rusk had telephoned to ask if she would like to audition for the Shakespeare Bay Company's summer festival. They were planning to do *Romeo and Juliet* that year, he said, and they would be taking on a few newcomers, fresh out of college like her, for the small roles. He had also hinted that if her audition went particularly well, she might have a shot at understudying the lead.

On the one hand, she had counted her blessings. Noel, as her godfather, was aware of her aspirations and had been thoughtful enough to set up this audition. It was a marvelous piece of luck for a young actress with no professional background.

On the other hand, the test that lay ahead of her that afternoon was formidable. Noel, as the artistic

head of the Shakespeare Bay Company, was legendary for his perfectionism. He had founded the
theater, guided it through twenty successful seasons to
its current level of prestige and continued to personally oversee the company's hiring of every actor, director, stagehand and secretary. He might have been
bringing Rebecca in for the audition because of a
family bond, but she wouldn't get a job unless she met
his high standards. Thus she felt doubly bound—to do
her godfather Noel proud and to impress the vener-
able Mr. Rusk with the soliloquy from *Romeo and
Juliet* she had prepared....

" 'Thou knowst the mask of night is on my
face—' "

A trio of horns blared from behind, startling her
and alerting her to the fact that the light had indeed
changed. Beneath her touch the ancient VW shivered
and lurched forward into the traffic, snaking its way
along the main street of Sausalito.

"Else would a maiden blush bepaint my cheek
For that which thou hast heard me speak
tonight...."

She had gone over those lines until she felt as if they
were etched upon her brain. She had chanted them in
the shower, mumbled them over the stove, dreamed
them at night. That morning she had awakened with
them on her lips.

" 'Fain would I dwell on form....' "

The words came out now in a husky whisper. Rebecca swallowed to relieve the lump in her throat and
prayed that 'her voice would not fail her at the last
minute. After all, Noel's was not the only significant
vote on the panel waiting to hear her speak those lines.
There was another important person whose approval
she must win: Nick Corelli, the man Noel had chosen
to direct *Romeo and Juliet*.

At thirty-three, Nick Corelli was fast becoming one

of the hottest young directors in the world. Only the week before, *Time* had run a gushing story on him in the "Theater" section, lavishly illustrated with various production stills and one enigmatic portrait of the man himself, hidden beneath a hat, sunglasses and the upturned collar of a trenchcoat. Who was he, Rebecca wondered, this camera-shy person who had hits running in Rome and London, and who had just received a Tony nomination for his New York production of *The Taming of the Shrew*.

About his personal life, there had been only a few lines, hinting that he was a loner yet linking his name with those of several young actresses and one prima ballerina. The bulk of the article had been devoted to an appraisal of his work, which it insisted was nothing short of genius. His direction was characterized as flamboyant, emotional and lucid. Under his hand, even the most well-known classics acquired such fresh rambunctious life that the audiences were constantly surprised by the productions. "Nick Corelli clearly regards Shakespeare as a living playwright...."

Yes, Noel had accomplished something of a coup by luring Corelli to Shakespeare Bay for the summer.

" 'Fain, fain deny what I have spoke....' "

Preoccupied with her lines, Rebecca came very close to driving past the old, two-story brick building that housed the offices and rehearsal rooms of the Shakespeare Bay Company. This converted warehouse was the hub of all activity until the latter stages of rehearsal when the production moved up the road to a beautiful outdoor amphitheater. Rebecca and her brother, Adam, had been invited to the past summer's gala opening of *A Midsummer Night's Dream* in this woodsy setting with the Milky Way stretching overhead. She had spent the whole evening secretly fantasizing about what it would be like to perform there.

" 'But farewell compliment....' "

Directly in front of the theater was an empty parking space. Rebecca couldn't believe her good luck. Parking in this part of Sausalito was always an ordeal and, according to her watch, she was cutting it much too close to spend any extra time searching for a spot. Perhaps this was an omen that everything might go well after all. In her excitement, she narrowly avoided a collision with a boy on a bicycle, then pulled up at last and prepared to back into the empty space. Calm down, she told herself, one thing at a time. . . .

" 'Dost thou love me?' "

The VW wobbled into reverse, shuddered, choked and died beneath her. With a cry of exasperation, she endeavored to start it again, but it was no use. She knew from experience that she would have to wait a full minute before the engine would oblige her by turning over.

In that minute, a sleek black Porsche slid deftly into the parking space.

"Hey!" she yelled through the open window. "That was mine!" Panicking at the thought of missing her appointment, she beeped twice for emphasis.

The tall bearded man who stepped out of the sports car looked at her as if she had lost her mind. "I beg your pardon?" he queried.

"I was here first!" Rebecca insisted hotly. "You just stole my parking space!"

"I did nothing of the kind," the stranger retorted coolly as he locked the car door behind him. "I saw you. You were double-parked. Now, please. Excuse me."

"Just a minute!" Rebecca scrambled out of the stalled VW in a mounting fury. It was as if all the anxiety and the pressure of the past two weeks had suddenly burst open in her chest and now came rushing out of her mouth in a torrent of angry words. "Excuse *me*! But I'm in a terrible hurry! I'm afraid you'll just have to move your car!" She slammed the door shut on the hem of her skirt, stepped forward and promptly lost her balance.

The dark-haired man rushed over to break her fall. "Careful!" he cried, catching her by the shoulders. She instinctively grabbed his arm for support as her head struck his chest. The rough wool of his sweater grazed her cheek and, suddenly dizzy, she leaned heavily against him. For a split second, she was mesmerized by something indefinable. *He smells marvelous,* she thought. *He smells like—*

"Are you all right?" he demanded, breaking her train of thought and helping her to right herself. "Look at this, *idiota*, you've caught your dress in the door." He opened it and quickly helped to free her skirts. "Now what is it that you want?"

"I want you to move your car," she insisted stubbornly, struggling to recover her lost dignity. "And I am *not* an idiot. . . ."

The man stepped away and fixed her with a penetrating stare. Rebecca was taken aback by the fire in his dark eyes and the contained strength of his presence. He was quite remarkable-looking: straight black hair falling carelessly forward in a lock on his brow; a dark, well-trimmed beard; broad shoulders, powerful beneath a white, cable-knit sweater. The corners of his mouth twitched slightly as if he didn't know whether to be amused or to match her temper for temper. "My dear lady," he began in a low resonant voice laced with mockery, "I saw you drive up. You're a hazard to the roads. You nearly ran over a boy on a bike. Then you double-park in the middle of a busy street. Now you pick a fight with me over a parking space you were making no attempt to use. . . until I drove up. What is your problem?"

"My problem is you!" Rebecca retorted, riled by his tone. "You must have seen my car stall. You zipped in and took advantage of the situation. It was a rude thing to do and I insist that you move!"

"Look at this. You're causing a traffic jam!" The man glanced about impatiently as a line of cars, thwarted by the obstruction of the VW, began to loudly sound their disapproval. "Take my advice. Go and call a tow truck and get that catastrophe of a car off the streets." He made a disdainful gesture with the back of his hand in the direction of the VW.

"But I—"

"Enough! I'm not moving and that's that. I've wasted too much time already." His eyes swept over her in a final rakish glance. "You're a pretty thing but you are the most awful driver. Now, I'm a busy man and I'm late." Without further ado, he turned his back on her and walked away.

"*Idioto!*" Rebecca called after him in a voice that would have no trouble reaching the last row of a large amphitheater. "Rude person!"

THERE HAD BEEN NO NEED to hurry, she learned upon arriving at the front office, breathless from a five-block race from her car back to Shakespeare Bay. The auditions were running a half hour behind schedule. Why didn't she take a seat, have some coffee and they would call her when they were ready? The secretary had smiled apologetically and shown Rebecca to the actors' "greenroom," a lounge filled with worn over-stuffed furniture and brightened by hanging plants and a colorful cluttered bulletin board.

Some of the other actors were standing around gossiping. Two intense young men were practicing fencing positions with imaginary swords. Another leaned against the doorway, his face buried in a text of the play, oblivious to the pandemonium around him. And there was a noticeable abundance of romantic-looking young women—blond, brunet, redheaded. The name "Juliet" was all but stamped upon their respective foreheads. This was the competition. Rebecca sighed. There were enough Juliets here to cast the role and its understudy a dozen times over.

Feeling somewhat overwhelmed, she took advantage of the delay to slip into the ladies' room and fix her disheveled hair, which had come undone from its chignon during her race to the theater. Besides, the privacy gave her a chance to recover her wits after that ludicrous encounter with the owner of the black Porsche. Each long rhythmic stroke of the brush soothed her frayed nerves. She was embarrassed— haggling like that over something as banal as a parking space. That bearded fellow would be surprised to learn that she was normally a rather shy person.

She brushed and brushed until her hair crackled with electricity. Long and black and full of lights, it fell in a rippling silky mass around her shoulders. Rebecca gave herself an appraising glance in the mirror and wrinkled her nose. She knew she was, well, attractive enough for all normal purposes—wasn't that the way her brother had phrased it?—but in her estimation she had nothing special. It was certainly not the face of any of the sophisticated leading ladies she currently admired.

In truth, she was unaware of her own loveliness. Her young face was at once both strong and delicate. She had bold, high cheekbones, but the soft, full mouth was as tender and as tremulous as a flower. Fine-boned and long-limbed, her willowy frame was animated by a vitality and a stubbornness of spirit.

Yet her eyes were her most arresting feature and made her beauty unique. Large and almond-shaped with irises of a light, light blue, they spoke of mystery and other-worldliness. They were the eyes of a dreamer.

In one quick gesture, Rebecca twisted her hair into a coil at her nape and pinned it into place. Despite all her misgivings, she was determined to see this audition through. One didn't have to have an Equity card or a long résumé, she told herself firmly, to behave in a professional manner.

When she checked the list on the bulletin board, it was apparent from the column of crossed-off names that there was still one person ahead of her. Someone named Chris Matheson.

"He just went in," a husky voice remarked over her shoulder, "and I wouldn't be surprised if he gets the part."

Rebecca turned to face a tall auburn-haired woman, very striking and somehow intimidating. "What part?" she asked blankly.

"Romeo, obviously." The woman chuckled. "Didn't you see him? All sort of lyrical and gorgeous. He's obviously up for Romeo."

"No, I didn't. See him," Rebecca murmured.

"I'm Evany Pace." The woman extended her hand with the firm assurance of a diva, startling Rebecca by the almost masculine pressure of her grip. "Who are you?"

"I'm Rebecca Yates."

"Yates? I don't believe I'm familiar with your work. . . ." Evany's beautiful face assumed a quizzical expression. "Are you from New York? L.A.?"

"I grew up in northern California. Mendocino." Rebecca found herself apologizing. "You don't know my work because it's all been in college theater."

"Well. . . ." Evany gave her a vague look. "That's sweet." She looked distractedly around the room. "Rebecca, do you have any smokes? I'm simply dying for a cigarette and I don't have a single one left."

"I'm afraid not. I don't smoke."

Evany regarded her drolly. "Very wise. Very sweet and very wise. It's a wicked habit. But then I'm full of wicked habits." She smiled bewitchingly. "It's true. I'm addicted to cigarettes. I'm addicted to applause. I'm addicted to good-looking men. . . ."

"Have you worked with Shakespeare Bay before?" Rebecca inquired, somewhat bewildered by the conversation.

"Last summer. I played Titania in *A Midsummer Night's Dream*. You know, the fairy queen. It was wonderful. I had a sparkly little costume cut up to here and down to there and I nearly froze my whatsit off in that amphitheater on cold nights." Evany uttered a deep throaty laugh that attracted the attention of everyone in the greenroom. "Oh, the perils of being a Shakespearean sex symbol!" she moaned deliciously as she and Rebecca were quickly joined by two young men.

"I saw your performance," Rebecca said. "You were very good."

"Yes, you were," echoed one of the young men, his boyish face alight with eagerness. "I saw the show three times."

"Now, aren't you wonderful!" Evany crooned, placing one languorous arm around his shoulders. "You don't happen to have any smokes, do you? I'm simply dying for a cigarette."

"Sure." The young man hastened to accommodate her as his friend fumbled in his pockets for matches. "Say, which part are you reading for today, Evany?"

She gave him a long look full of smoldering scorn. "Which part do you think? I'm reading for the lead." Then she smiled and accepted the cigarette. "I can't help it. I'm addicted to leading roles. And in another year or two, I'll be too old to play Juliet." Evany paused, her gray eyes sparkling as she exhaled the smoke with a long sigh of pleasure. "Besides, I'd give my right...knee to work with Nick Corelli."

"Miss Yates?" the secretary interrupted. "They're ready for you now."

Rebecca's heart leaped into her throat. "Well," she said, excusing herself to the group, "it was very nice to meet you."

"Goodbye, Ramona," Evany said, smiling. "I'm sure you'll do well."

"REBECCA, MY DEAR!" Noel exclaimed merrily as he came forward to greet her. "How good of you to come and see us today." At sixty, he was still a most elegant figure, angular of face, with a lean elongated frame. Ten years as an actor, twelve as a director, and the past twenty as producer of Shakespeare Bay had given him an unusual strength of presence. His hair had gone completely white in recent years, but his sea-blue eyes were as bright and as sharp as they had ever been. Despite her awe of him, Rebecca had a great affection for her godfather. The times they had spent together had been few and far between but always filled with a special warmth. "Now, come and meet everyone!" he said, taking her hand in his and leading her across the cool high-ceilinged rehearsal hall to where a group of men sat behind a long table. "I hope we haven't kept you waiting too long?"

"No, not at all," Rebecca murmured as her heart fluttered wildly in her chest. This was it. This was what she had been waiting for. Two weeks of anticipation, trepidation and high excitement had finally brought her to this moment.

Noel was busily making the introductions. "The fellow on your left is Danny Garret, my assistant who helps us with all the casting here at Shakespeare Bay." Rebecca reached out and blindly shook the hand offered her. "And the man in the funny hat," Noel continued charmingly, endeavoring to put her at her ease, "is Harry Moss, production stage manager." Another handshake. "And finally, Nick Corelli, who'll be directing *Romeo and Juliet* for us." Rebecca held out her hand but could not bring herself to lift her eyes, so deep was her sense of fright. Thus, she was thoroughly shocked when the man held on to her hand, drew it to his lips and softly kissed the back of it.

Rebecca gasped, pulled quickly back and found herself looking into a pair of familiar fiery dark eyes. It was he. The monster of the black Porsche. Nick Corelli. "Oh, no..." she whispered as she flushed a deep shade of crimson.

Mr. Corelli was looking mightily entertained. "Rebecca and I have already met," he told Noel.

Noel was surprised. "Oh, yes?"

"Yes," Nick assured him. "We waged the War of Roses over a parking space in front of the theater. I won, but Rebecca put up a good fight.'' He grinned. ''It was the sort of encounter I frequently enjoy in New York, but out here in California I thought you people were supposed to be—what is the word?—mellow.''

''Mellow,'' Noel repeated, amused. ''Laid back.''

''Well, anyway,'' Noel continued, ''if Rebecca can work up that much passion over a parking space, I'm sure she can spare a little for Romeo.'' The other men chuckled. Rebecca wanted to throttle them all, especially the provoking Mr. Corelli. ''Have you brought us a picture and résumé?'' Nick inquired.

''Yes, I have.'' Rebecca handed it to him, glad to get back to business. ''I'm afraid the picture isn't very good, but it's the only one I have.''

Nick held it out in front of him, looked at Rebecca for a long moment and then back at the photograph. ''It's not bad. But it doesn't do you justice. Who took it?''

''My brother.''

''Ah,'' he said with a nod, smiling. ''Well. He's captured that side of you a brother would see.''

''What do you mean?'' she asked, uncomprehending.

''He's caught that aspect of you which is a young girl, a lovely little sister...rather than a woman. It's very nice, but you'll have to get other pictures someday.'' He turned the sheet over and glanced at her résumé on the back. ''You've done some Shakespeare, I see.''

''Yes, in college.''

''Queen Margaret in *Richard III*. Very impressive. Queen Margaret is supposed to be a hundred and ten. How did you manage it?'' He could barely suppress his amusement.

''Well, you see, in college, everyone is young,'' she hastened to explain. ''One winds up playing all kinds of parts.''

''I know just what you mean.'' Noel came to her

rescue. "Long ago, when I was in boarding school—it was all boys of course—I was cast as Cleopatra. And I was very good, too, I might add."

Nick was continuing to scrutinize her with his burning eyes. She felt herself go warm beneath his gaze. It was as if he saw everything—every telltale gesture, every feature, every thought. She was most uncomfortable.

"So," he spoke at last, "we have here a picture of a young girl and the résumé of an old character actress. Perhaps Rebecca will allow us to see what lies between. What piece are you going to do for us today?"

"It's one of Juliet's speeches."

"Very good. Why don't you step out there where we can all see you and begin whenever you're ready."

For one wild moment, she considered walking out of the room and never coming back. Performing had always been a great source of pleasure—when the role belonged solely to her and the audience sat just beyond the circle of lights, invisible, uncritical and ready to be entertained. But auditioning was another story. Four pairs of eyes were silently watching, waiting to judge her talent. And she could see every feature on Nick Corelli's arrogant handsome face. Her legs quickly turned to water and her brain to mush.

But there was no turning back now. She wouldn't give Corelli the satisfaction.

"'Thou knowst the mask of night is on my face. . . .'"

The lines came out in a soft whispery voice. Rebecca reached deep inside herself for all the courage she had and continued with her speech. The lines flowed naturally, and by the end she was able to hit some of the emotional notes she had so painstakingly rehearsed. At last it was over and she couldn't help releasing a deep sigh of relief. It had gone better that morning in the shower, to be sure; but at least she had got through it without disgrace. She raised her head and looked over at Nick Corelli.

He nodded. "That was fine. You speak the verse quite well."

Rebecca couldn't believe her ears. Was this praise? From the monster?

"But now I'd like to try something else, with your permission," he continued, getting up from his chair and crossing to where she stood. "I'd like to work with you a little bit, just to see how you respond to direction. I'll give you a few suggestions and you'll do the speech again for me, all right?"

Rebecca nodded.

"First of all...." He was staring at her again, hands on his hips, his head cocked to one side in concentration. "Can you take your hair down? That wouldn't be too difficult, would it?" He gestured questioningly at the chignon at the back of her head.

"No," Rebecca murmured, surprised by his request. "I can do that." She reached hesitatingly for the pins.

"Juliet is getting ready for bed, is she not? She steps outside onto the balcony of her room to look at the stars and remember the exciting young man she danced with earlier at the ball. When Romeo appears suddenly in the garden beneath her, she is startled, embarrassed...." Nick reached out and shook the dark coil of hair loose around her shoulders. She felt something within her flutter wildly as his fingers accidently brushed her cheek. "Romeo's caught her half-undressed," he continued. "And he's just overheard everything she's said about him." She could hear the excitement in Nick's voice as he described the scene to her. It was as if he were communicating his vision to her on some visceral level. "Juliet may go through many feelings in the course of this speech. She's confused; she's aroused; she's giddy with excitement." Suddenly Rebecca felt herself catch fire. It was as if some spark had leaped from Nick to her.

He saw it. "Good, good," he murmured, retreating to one side and leaving her alone in the center of the room. "And I don't want to hear a quiet little voice. I want that full passionate voice I heard down in the street."

Rebecca flushed from the tips of her toes to the roots of her hair.

"That's it!" Nick cried. "That's the beginning of the scene. Now, let's have the lines. . . ."

"Thou knowst the mask of night is on my face.
Else would a maiden blush bepaint my cheek
For that which thou hast heard me speak
tonight. . . ."

Her cheeks were on fire. Her voice came pouring out now, dark and husky. The rehearsal hall receded. She was in an orchard. The air was fragrant. It was a summer night and she was talking to her lover. She laughed. She felt herself tremble with desire. She sailed through the speech and suddenly, much too soon, it was over. The man in the corner was not Romeo, but Nick Corelli. His expression was indecipherable. "*Bene*. Good," he said quietly. "Thank you for coming in."

"Very well done, my dear," Noel put in. "We'll be getting in touch with you as soon as we know what's what."

Rebecca murmured a goodbye and left the room in a kind of haze, not at all sure what had just happened to her.

ON THE DRIVE HOME from the theater, the entire world looked somehow different. Outside, it was a rapturous, sky-blue, gull-white Sausalito day, but she had been much too preoccupied to notice it before. This picturesque little waterfront community was a mere fifteen-minute ride north over the Golden Gate Bridge from San Francisco, and today the sidewalks were

thronged with sightseers. There were couples everywhere. Hand in hand, they strolled along the yacht
harbor, browsed past the quaint shop windows on
Bridgeway, spilled laughingly out of the restaurants
and saloons onto the narrow village streets. It was
just that sort of balmy Saturday afternoon in late
spring that was made for lovers. The bay was a riot
of sailboats. Across the glittering water, the white
skyline of San Francisco rose like an elaborate daydream.

Freed at last from the weight of her impending audition, Rebecca felt her heart grow as light as the salty
sea breeze that floated through the open window of
the car. She shook her head happily and let the dark
web of hair ripple out behind her.

What had happened to her back in that rehearsal
hall had been disturbing, exhilarating and...there
was something she couldn't quite put her finger on.
She had never met a director like Nick Corelli before.
She had certainly never felt that way on a stage before.
The scene had come welling out of her, immediate and
full. And it was Nick who had brought her to this new
and surprising experience. It was almost as if he had
made love to her.

Rebecca blushed at the thought, as a host of images
and impressions flooded back into her mind. Those
piercing dark eyes. The vibrancy of his fingers in her
hair. The unique tantalizing scent of him whenever he
stood in close proximity.

And yet they had been in a room with three other
people. It had all been part of a formal process. The
contact had been professional—not personal.

She was mystified.

Turning at last onto Gate Five Road, the entrance to
Sausalito's houseboat colony, she pulled in beside a
familiar yellow pickup truck and parked. Her brother
had obviously arrived before her. Adam had arranged
for Rebecca to sublet a vacationing friend's houseboat
for the summer, though he continued to voice his con-

cern over her decision to live alone for the first time. He was her only family, after all.

Adam had been twenty-three and Rebecca nine the summer their parents had died. Mr. and Mrs. Yates had been returning from San Francisco to their Mendocino ranch along the fog-bound Pacific Coast Highway when their car skidded off the winding road and crashed onto the rocks below, instantly killing them both. After the funeral, Adam had insisted upon assuming complete responsibility for his sister, refusing to relinquish her to any of the aunts or cousins who offered to be her guardian. He had driven her to school, bought her clothes, taught her to cook and given her little jobs helping to groom and care for the horses that he raised. Life on the ranch had made her solitary, self-sufficient and somewhat naive in the ways of the world.

It was a good thing, she thought as she walked along the pier to the spot where the houseboat was moored, this decision to move to Sausalito, at least for the summer. She was twenty-one now and it was high time she tried living by herself, free to make her own choices and her own mistakes. It would be good for Adam, too. She had always harbored a guilty feeling that he had neglected his own life to create a home for her. Shy and good-hearted, he was still unmarried at thirty-five and showed every indication of becoming an eccentric old bachelor.

The houseboat belonging to Adam's friend, Perry Jens, was connected to the middle of the pier by a narrow gangplank with railings on each side. Perry had built the houseboat himself, and it reflected the workings of his unique imagination. A small, fantastical geometric puzzle, the boat had a center section housing a long, rectangular living room that was flanked by octagons. One octagon was the kitchen; the other, the bedroom and bath. In the back, sliding glass doors opened out on to a semicircular deck where one could sun, read or even, conceivably, fish.

Rebecca found her brother in the kitchen, stocking the refrigerator with food from two brown paper bags beside him on the floor. "I brought the rest of the stuff you wanted from the ranch," he told her. "And I stopped along the way and picked up a few groceries."

"You're too much," she said with a laugh, kissing him on the cheek. "You think I'm going to starve the minute I'm out from under your roof. Now, come on, how much do I owe you for all this?"

Adam gave her his slow, shy cowboy smile. "Nothing."

"Adam! I told you I'm planning to support myself from now on."

"Well, you better wait till you get the job," he drawled, scratching his head and looking at her with a twinkle in his eye. "Then you can support me."

Rebecca chuckled. He was funny, this brother of hers. And nice-looking, too: tall and lanky with a shock of brown hair and light blue eyes like her own. She hoped he'd meet someone nice now that she was no longer underfoot.

"Well, Becca, you gonna keep me in suspense?" he demanded, opening a can of beer. "How did it go? You remember your lines?"

"Yes...." She hesitated as she poured herself a glass of apple juice.

"Well?"

"Well, it was strange. I don't quite know how to tell you...."

"Come on, let's sit out on the deck. This place is giving me cabin fever."

Outside, the sun had begun to sink low in the sky. All around them the other houseboats creaked and groaned, emitting strains of music and the homey smell of suppers on the stove. Gulls circled overhead and swooped, ever on the lookout for food. In the distance, the tall bare masts of the sailboats, moored down for the night, swayed like a forest of bamboo.

"Adam, I've got to do something about the VW!"

she remembered suddenly as she settled into a canvas lounge chair.

"What's the matter with it?" he asked. "I spent four hours working on the engine last week."

"It makes me crazy," she told him emphatically, chagrined by the memory. "It stalled right in front of the theater. There was a traffic jam. I got into a fight with the director...only I didn't find out he was the director until later. It was mortifying."

"I'll take it to a garage. In the meantime, Perry's left a bike in one of the closets."

"I'll use that, then. As long as I leave in plenty of time."

"Becca, honey," Adam began tentatively, "what if you don't get this job?"

"If they won't let me act, then I'll work in the box office, run errands, whatever," she retorted defiantly. "But I think the audition went well."

"Good. I'm glad. Don't bite my head off, will you?" Adam raised his hands over his head in mock protest. "Maybe you'll even be the star."

"I don't think there's any chance of that." She laughed, suddenly shy. "But maybe I'll get to be a lady-in-waiting and understudy the star."

"This director liked you then?"

"I don't know." She felt herself begin to flush. "He...he did work with me a little bit, so...."

"So he must have thought you had something to offer." Adam noticed the change in his sister's manner. "What's he like?"

"Oh...Italian, I think, though he doesn't have an accent. Very intense. Very bright."

"Young?"

"Oh, no!" she responded gravely. "Old. At least your age."

"Ancient!" Adam chuckled. "Ancient and funny-looking. Did he have a wart on his nose by any chance?"

"No!" She hit him playfully. "He's not...funny-looking."

"Good-looking?"

"Oh. . . ." She sighed audibly and nodded her head.

"*Very* good-looking?"

"Oh, stop it!" she demanded, annoyed. "What does it matter anyway?"

Adam stood up and kissed the top of her head. "Be careful, Becca. Promise me you'll be careful."

"I don't know what you're talking about." She folded her arms tightly across her chest. "Where are you going?"

"To take a look at the VW before it gets any darker outside. Then I'll come back and take you out for Chinese food before I drive back to Mendocino."

"Fine," she said, nodding.

"By the way, Perry says the woman in the next houseboat also works at Shakespeare Bay Company. If worse comes to worst, maybe you can catch a ride in with her. Name's Maggie something."

"I'll remember that."

After he had gone, she sat there for some time, relaxing and drinking in the colorful sights of this unique community where she would be living. All around her floated houseboats of every conceivable shape and size. One was drum-shaped, its sides painted with hieroglyphics and mysterious Egyptian figures. Another, the *Fortune Cookie*, looked like something from an Oriental painting. Some sported cupolas with stained-glass windows. Others were surrounded on all sides by decks, decorated with cacti, flower boxes, seashells and driftwood. Next door, the *SS Maggie* rose two stories high, sleek and elegant with skylights and a shingled roof.

At last Rebecca rose reluctantly and drifted into the bedroom to begin unpacking the half-dozen boxes Adam had brought from the ranch. On the bed in an open suitcase, Perry's pet, Samcat, had curled up among her clothes for a snooze. "Shoo," she told him, "get out of there." The great, tiger-striped, battle-scarred animal looked at her with his one good eye and purred.

Before she could evict him, the phone rang and she hurried to answer it. Probably some friend of Perry's wondering where he'd gone. She was surprised when a resonant male voice asked, "May I speak with Miss Yates, please?"

"This is she."

"Oh, good. Miss Yates, this is Nick Corelli. I was about to give up on you. My secretary's been calling you for the past few hours."

"My brother and I were sitting outside," she managed to say, as her heart did a flipflop in her chest. "I didn't hear the phone."

"Well, I'm glad I caught you before we all went home. I'd like you to come in again at eleven-thirty on Monday morning and read with Chris Matheson, who'll be playing Romeo for us. Can you do that?"

She had to sit down on the bed and catch her breath before she answered. "Yes. Yes, of course."

"Very good. We'll see you then."

And he was gone, without so much as a goodbye. Rebecca sat with the receiver in her hand for several minutes before she regained the presence of mind to hang up. She lay back on the bed, pressed both palms to her eyes and sighed. She had been called back. He wanted to see her again.

She rolled luxuriously to one side and stroked Samcat's fur. He climbed out of the suitcase and curled up beside her ingratiatingly. Rebecca closed her eyes and saw again the dark gaze, the sensuous mouth, the strong sensitive hands. And what was that elusive scent she could never quite put a name to?

Then it came to her. As a child, she had loved to dig in the black soil of Adam's vegetable garden. It had seemed to her to be a magic substance. Moist and dark and rich, it was capable of producing the most amazing variety of things—food and flowers, trees and grass.

Underneath his expensive cologne, Nick Corelli had the rich and loamy smell of earth.

CHAPTER TWO

REBECCA ARRIVED at the theater a half hour early Monday morning, determined to show Nick Corelli that she was a responsible actress and not some harum-scarum, accident-prone girl. There would be no repeat of Saturday's parking fiasco. She chained the bike to a pole in front of the building and carefully smoothed a few wrinkles out of the calf-length, flared, cotton skirt she had chosen to wear. She hoped the boots and the delicate knit sweater would help to give her a soft, quasi-Shakespearean look. After all, Juliet could hardly wear jeans.

Coming into the theater out of the bright sunlight, Rebecca inadvertently bumped into a man standing just inside the entranceway. "Excuse me," she murmured.

The man looked at her. As the devil would have it, it was Nick Corelli. "Not at all," he said, somewhat slightly distracted by the interruption. From the look of things, he had been deeply engrossed in a conversation with Evany Pace. Ms Pace, resplendent in a pale violet silk dress, lounged against the balustrade of a staircase, one hand resting proprietorily upon Nick's arm. She looked pleased, excited, her gray eyes luminous beneath thick lashes.

Rebecca ducked her head and continued walking.

"Miss Yates," he called after her.

She turned around.

"Pick up a copy of the play from my secretary and look over the balcony scene, will you?" His voice was cool, businesslike. "I'll be with you in a little while."

A few minutes later, as she curled up with the script in a greenroom chair, she found herself wondering if perhaps Evany had already been cast in the lead role. That might account for the pleased expression and her newfound intimacy with Nick. Or perhaps they had begun seeing each other. Rebecca shook her head and shrugged. What business of hers was it, anyway?

Yet... what if she were assigned to understudy Evany for the summer? The thought gave her a little chill. What would it be like attending rehearsals, memorizing Evany's every gesture, watching Evany perform this magnificent role under Nick Corelli's tutelage, while she, Rebecca, sat in the dark at the back of the theater, extraneous and ignored? There was no doubt about it; the understudy was a kind of Cinderella—given lots of hard work but not allowed to go to the ball.

In that instant, she knew. What she really wanted was to play the role of Juliet herself. No matter that she had comparatively little experience. No matter that Nick and Noel had probably never considered her in that capacity. To pretend she would be happy with understudying was nothing but false humility. Well, if by some chance the role was still open, the least she could do was go in and give it her best shot. Then, even if she failed, she could be proud of herself for trying.

"Hi. Are you reading for Juliet?" A voice interrupted her furious train of thought.

Rebecca gazed up into a very appealing face, one that was strangely familiar in a way she couldn't quite put her finger on. The young man was tall and slim with fine, sensitively molded features. Dark blond hair, streaked by the sun. Brown eyes. There was a youthful sweetness about him. She was sure she had never met him, but wondered if she might have seen him in a play. Perhaps he, like Evany, was an alumnus of other summers at Shakespeare Bay. "Yes," she replied, as if announcing her new intention to the world, "I am reading for Juliet."

"Good. We'll be reading together," he told her cheerfully as he took the seat beside her. "I'm Chris Matheson."

"Oh!" She recognized the name. "I hear you're playing Romeo. Congratulations."

"Thanks." He grinned. "I was really happy to get the part."

"I'm Rebecca Yates."

"How are you, Rebecca?" He shook the hand she offered him. His grip was warm, gentle. *He's perfect for the role,* she thought to herself. *Evany was right.*

"I'm scared to death," she told him with a twinkle in her eye, "but other than that, I'm terrific."

He laughed and squeezed her hand reassuringly. "We're all scared, honey. It goes with the territory. And from where I'm sitting, yes, you *are* terrific."

"Well," she said with a smile, "thanks for making me feel like I'm not alone." How quickly he had put her at ease. She felt as comfortable with him as she did with Adam.

When the secretary summoned them to the audition hall, she was thankful for her new ally. Nick Corelli surveyed the pairing with some interest, his piercing gaze falling first on Rebecca, passing then to Chris and finally back to Rebecca. She returned his look without flinching or glancing shyly away as she had on the previous occasion. The action was not lost on him. He nodded and raised an eyebrow one infinitesimal degree.

"I trust you've had a chance to look over the scene," he addressed her at last.

"Yes, I have." The fact was she knew it by heart.

"Good." He took his seat at the end of the table with Noel and the two assistants. "I'd like to hear you read it once with Chris. I don't expect a full performance. I just want to hear how you sound together."

"All right." She smiled, aware of the slow surge of excitement building within her.

"And don't feel as if you have to rush. If you like,

you can take a moment to relax before you begin," he offered as he leaned forward onto his elbows. The man was like some great cat: intense, concentrated, lithe.

"I don't need a moment," she told him steadily. "I'm ready now."

The gesture of his hand indicated that the space was all hers.

Chris led her into the scene, easily, naturally. The bond of empathy they had established earlier in the greenroom now blossomed and supported them. It was like dancing with a partner you knew you could trust. Soon Rebecca ceased to look down at the script and relied only on memory. This was her chance and she was taking it. With a heady new sense of freedom, she found herself making bold choices—inventing movement, responding wholeheartedly to her partner, discovering moments of humor and of quiet. When at last it was over, she was breathless, flushed as if she had just run a race.

Nick's face held a most peculiar smile. "Well," he commented wryly, "I said I didn't expect a performance, but I got one anyway." He stepped forward and clasped her hand in his warm one. She felt a faint shiver run through her but struggled to suppress her reaction. There it was again, that thick and earthy aura that became palpable when he stood this close. "Thanks for coming in again, Rebecca," he told her. "We'll contact you when we've made a decision."

"Thank you," she said, taking back her hand before it began to tremble.

"Goodbye, my dear," Noel rose from his chair and escorted her to the door. "Now, if I were you, I'd take the rest of the day off and do something absolutely frivolous."

CHRIS MATHESON caught up with her just outside the theater and encouraged her to take Noel's suggestion to heart. "Let's have a picnic or something," he pleaded with a most beguiling smile. "I'm pretty good company and it'll be much better than sitting around waiting for your phone to ring." She had to agree, and before she knew it he had secured her bicycle to a rack on the back of his shiny green Volvo and whisked her down the street to a neighborhood deli, where he proceeded to buy far more than the two of them could possibly eat.

At her suggestion, they returned the bike to the houseboat and loaded their lunch into the dinghy that Perry kept tied to the rear deck. As they rowed out some distance from the houseboat colony, the bay was alive with ducks and pelicans, and the sky stretched overhead, blue and cloudless. At last, allowing the dinghy to drift in the mild currents, Chris uncorked a bottle of wine and insisted upon serving Rebecca the various delicacies he had chosen. Something in his manner and the way he moved continued to tickle her memory.

"Why do I feel as if I know you?" she asked him as she munched on a cracker spread with a delicious pâté. "Have you worked at Shakespeare Bay before?"

"No." He shook his head. "Have you?"

"Oh, no. As a matter of fact, I've never worked professionally."

"You could have fooled me," he said with a grin. "I hope you get the job."

"I hope it isn't already cast."

"I don't think it is. Why would they have you read if it were already cast?"

"For the understudy."

He shrugged and reached over to fill her glass with a sparkling rosé. "You're too pretty to be the understudy."

Rebecca laughed and looked away. She had never learned how to take a compliment. "You haven't answered my question you know," she reminded him.

"What question?" He seemed genuinely puzzled.

"Why do I feel as if I know you? Have I seen you in a play? Tell me."

"Oh. . . ." He shifted in his seat. Now it was his turn to be uncomfortable.

"Well?"

"You probably saw me in a television series," he mumbled, studying his sandwich as if it had suddenly become very interesting to him.

Rebecca was intrigued. "Which one?" she asked.

"My family and I were on a series called 'Our House' for almost nine years," he told her at last, though with some reluctance. "It was a half-hour comedy. My parents and my twin sisters and I played this sort of idealized American family. I was seven when I started working and almost sixteen when the show finally went off the air." He laughed and brushed the fair hair out of his eyes where the wind had blown it. "I literally grew up on that show."

"I don't believe this." Rebecca shook her head in amazement. "I had a terrible crush on you when I was fourteen. I cut your picture out of a magazine and carried it around in my wallet for months."

A smile broke over his face, which for some reason had grown strangely melancholy as he talked about the show. "Well, maybe it was worth it after all. . . ."

"What do you mean?" She cocked her head quizzically to one side. "It sounds like a wonderful experience!"

"It was. Wonderful in some ways, tough in others. But I'd rather hear about you." He tore the crust off his sandwich and tossed it to a passing duck. "Did you really cut out my picture? What did your boyfriend have to say about that?"

"Oh, I didn't have any boyfriends. I grew up on a ranch and it was very isolated. . . ." She proceeded to tell him all about her childhood in Mendocino, sensing that he had touched some pain within himself and preferred to leave the subject of his past alone. Chris listened raptly as if her life story was the most fascinating one he'd heard, and soon he was his sunny boyish self once more. At last, when the food was packed away and the sun had begun to sink low along the hills, they reluctantly pulled out the paddles and rowed back to the houseboat. Samcat was waiting for them at the edge of the deck.

"He's probably hungry," Rebecca told Chris as they secured the dinghy to its mooring. "Offer him that last little bit of tuna fish and see if he'll eat it."

The big tiger cat rose up on its back paws and embraced Chris's knee while he searched for the remains of the sandwich. "You're going to have a surprise a few weeks from now," Chris advised her as he stroked the animal's fur.

"What's that?" Rebecca asked over her shoulder. She was fumbling with the lock on the sliding glass doors leading into the living room.

"Samcat is a she. Samcat is going to present you with some kittens in the not-too-distant future."

"You're joking!" Rebecca's jaw fell open. One cat she was prepared to look after—but five or six? Before she could verify Chris's claim, she heard the phone ring in the bedroom and, flinging the door aside, she hurried to answer it.

"Rebecca?" The voice was one she instantly recognized. "This is Nick Corelli."

"Yes," she answered breathlessly. "Hello." Her heart had begun to pound against her ribs as she was filled with a curious mixture of dread and almost unbearable excitement.

"Noel and I have talked it over . . ." he began, then paused for a moment. She sank down on the edge of the bed and held her breath. "We've talked it over and we've decided to offer you the part. Are you interested?"

She wasn't sure if she had heard him correctly. "Uh-huh," she replied dumbly. "Which part?"

He sounded amused. "Which part do you think? Lady Macbeth. Are you interested?"

"Don't tease me," she told him. "I'm very nervous."

"The part of Juliet," he explained patiently.

"The understudy or the part?"

"The part."

"You want me to play the part?"

"Well, we did. Are you trying to talk us out of it?"

"No!" she exclaimed loudly, then muffled the receiver with her hand and valiantly tried to collect her wits. "No," she told him in a softer voice. "I accept."

"Good." He enunciated the word as if she were a harebrained child whose attention might wander at any moment. "Can you be here at three tomorrow to sign some contracts?"

"Yes," she said shakily. "Yes."

"That's three o'clock. Now I want you to write that down before I hang up."

She scrambled for paper and pen. "Three o'clock," she repeated. "I'll be there."

"I'll see you then." He chuckled, then abruptly hung up.

She returned the receiver to its cradle and stared at the piece of paper before her. For an instant she felt frozen, as if she dare not celebrate lest it all prove to be some terrible mistake. Then a wave of joy rose from the bottom of her feet and exploded in her chest. "Chris!" she cried, her voice echoing all over the houseboat. "Chris, I got the part!"

HER SIGNATURE LOOKED strangely unfamiliar when she saw it at the bottom of all those legal documents. In addition to the contracts, Noel had arranged for her to join the actors' union, offering to take the whopping initiation fee out of her paycheck over a period of time. "Does that look right to you?" she asked him dreamily as she handed back the forms. "Is that the way I usually spell my name?"

"Rebecca Yates. Rebecca Yates. Rebecca Yates." Noel checked over the papers, one by one, and winked at her. "Not a bad name for an actress."

"I'm lucky," she told him with a smile. "My moth-

er came very close to naming me after her Aunt Heph-
zibah.''

"I'm very proud of you, Becca." He took her hand
and held it for a moment between his two large ones.
"And I'm sure your parents would have been, too."
She was moved. Noel's approval meant a great deal to
her. "Nick," he called into the next office. "Is there
anything else we need this young lady for before we let
her go home?''

Nick appeared in the doorway, absorbed in arrang-
ing the pages of a typed script he held in his hand. She
was once again struck by his extraordinary appearance. It had made a strong but somewhat blurred
impression upon her during the auditions; now that
she was no longer under such intense scrutiny herself,
she was able to study him in more detail. The soft dark
hair and beard framed a face that was all the more un-
forgettable for its imperfection. The eyes were beautiful, deep-set and thickly lashed, lit from within by
some secret fire. At the corner of his left eye, curving
down his cheekbone, was a small but visible scar in the
shape of a crescent moon. The mouth was classical
and full, and could upon occasion twist upward into a
most disturbing smile, at once both mocking and sen-
sual. The Roman nose appeared to have been broken
in some long-ago accident and lent an agreeable
roughness to the whole.

He was dressed in his customary casual good taste;
well-cut tan slacks, a fine cotton shirt open at the
neck, a tweed jacket of classic proportions. The subtle elegance of his clothes contrasted arrestingly with
the sheer animal vitality of his physical being. It was
impossible not to notice how powerful and lithe he
was—like an athlete or a dancer. Everything about
him contributed to the impression of an unpredict-
able elemental force wonderfully veiled by a thin
layer of civilization. He slipped the loose pages into
a leather binder and handed it to Rebecca. "Rehearsal at ten in the morning," he told her. "And you

have an appointment with costumes tomorrow at five.''

"All right." She nodded, suddenly unable to think of anything to say. The man made her so hopelessly uncomfortable. "Well, I guess I'll be off then.''

"I'll walk out with you," he said, picking up a set of keys from Noel's desk. "I was about to leave myself.'' He stood to one side, allowing Rebecca to pass ahead of him through the open doorway.

"See you in the morning, Nick," Noel called after them. "Bye, Becca.''

"Goodbye," she replied in a singsong voice.

"What is this 'Becca'?" Nick asked her as they made their way down a long corridor to the front door.

"A family nickname," she told him. "My brother and Noel call me that.''

"Ah yes, Noel is your godfather. He didn't tell me that until after you were cast, you know. Just so you don't think there was any nepotism involved," he added teasingly as he opened the door for her and together they stepped out into the golden sunlight of the late afternoon. "Tell me, are you still driving that disastrous automobile?''

"Not at the moment," she replied, her eyes narrowing at the mockery in his tone. "Today I walked.''

"Very admirable of you." He paused beside the door of the black Porsche, which was now parked in the identical spot they had fought over only a few days ago. "But, as I'm sure you're exhausted from signing all those contracts, perhaps you'd like a ride? Becca?''

She found herself smiling at his use of her nickname. "Yes, all right," she agreed. "If it's not out of your way.''

"Actually, I was about to take a drive over to the amphitheater," he said, helping her into the front seat. "Would you like to come along and check out the stage?''

The idea was too tempting to resist. She had only

visited the place before as a member of the audience. How different might it all seem from center stage? "I'd love to," she told him. He nodded agreeably, leaned over to fasten her seat belt, and they were off.

The road to the amphitheater was a winding fifteen-minute drive along the slopes of Mount Tamalpais, which rose like a great earthen sentinel over Sausalito, Mill Valley and most of Marin County. Nick elected to take it at top speed. Rebecca's heart leaped into her throat as they made a dizzying ascent through forests of redwood trees, flew over hairpin curves with drop-offs yawning on one side and passed fellow motorists as casually as if they were barely there. "For God's sake, slow down!" she said when she could no longer contain herself. "Are you crazy?"

He glanced over at her and laughed. There was a wild light dancing in his eyes as he skillfully maneuvered the car around another snakelike bend in the road. This recklessness was the very quality she had intuitively known lay buried somewhere beneath his cosmopolitan veneer. Now it flared forth, frightening her. Nick Corelli was surely a madman.

"This car is like a fine racehorse," he told her. "You can't drive it as if it were a mule."

"No," she retorted. "But you can stop and let me out!" Ever since her parents' accident, she had harbored a fear of high speeds and dangerous roads.

"Don't be silly," he replied, dismissing her protests. "We're almost there. Trust me."

The road opened out suddenly onto a sunny slope overlooking the Pacific Ocean, which stretched in a blue and shimmering expanse as far as the eye could see. Rebecca held her breath and covered her mouth with the back of her hand. Nightmare images flashed through her head. Then suddenly the road curved once more into a grove of eucalyptus trees.

Nick took note of a slow-moving van, rumbling along just ahead of them, gunned the accelerator and swung out around the offending vehicle. Two sets of horns screamed out a warning. Rebecca looked up in horror to see a mammoth tour bus bearing down upon them in the oncoming lane and was sure her short life was just about to come to an end. Nick sailed back in just ahead of the van, narrowly avoiding a collision. The expression on his face was as blithe as if he had just won a round of some favorite sport. At last he pulled into a wide, gravel-filled shoulder and stopped. "Still with me?" he asked, reaching over to tousle her hair playfully.

She gave him a look of outrage and pushed away his hand. "You may not give a damn about your own life," she told him furiously, "but you have no right to risk mine!"

He drew back to observe her with his penetrating gaze. "Wonderful," he commented, stroking his beard with one hand as if he were very pleased about something. "Look at you—hair flying, eyes ablaze, trembling with emotion. I knew you had a wonderful temper. Now, that's exactly the way Juliet should look in act 3, scene 2. . . ."

She couldn't believe what she was hearing. The man had almost killed them both and all he could think about was his *play*. Was he even human? "Right now, I couldn't care less how Juliet looks," she retorted. "I'm not talking about fantasy. I'm talking about life! Do you know how treacherous this road can be? Do you know how many cars have gone off it and down the side of the mountain?"

"Bambina," he said soothingly. "I've never had an accident in my life. Now how many drivers can tell you that?"

"The way you drive, one accident is all it would take!" Her hands were still shaking, and she could feel her eyes beginning to tear belatedly.

"Now come, Becca, that will never happen—"

"It can happen! I lost both my parents in an accident on a road not so very different from this one!"

Now he was truly sorry. "Forgive me, I didn't

know." He reached over and caressed her cheek. She turned sharply away from him. He made an attempt to put his arm around her shoulders, but she would have none of it. Finally he caught her hand and refused to release it despite her protests. "Look," he said, "I promise never to drive fast when you are in the car. You may set the pace." He laughed softly. "I'm an arrogant man and that's a very big concession. Now do you forgive me?"

She looked back at him and slowly nodded her head. He leaned forward and kissed the corner of her eye where one large unshed tear hovered precariously. "Good," he said and kissed the other eye for good measure. She caught her breath and looked down at her lap, suddenly confused by his proximity.

"You think I was cruel just now," he continued, stroking her cheek lightly with his forefinger, "to relate your personal distress to the role you are about to play. But if you are going to be an actress, you must learn to do just that. You must be able to observe and remember everything that happens to you. One part of you may be crying, but in your head some other part is taking notes."

She scrunched up her nose in distaste. "It sounds so unnatural—"

"No," he insisted, looking deeply into her eyes to make sure she was comprehending him. "It's a blessing. It will allow you to take all the rage and frustration and pain you may have suffered and turn them into gold." He brought the back of her hand to his lips briefly and then released it. "Come on—" he smiled as he opened the door "—let's go and see the stage."

She was still mulling over his advice as she followed him down the wooded path that led to the amphitheater. He was so contradictory, this Nick Corelli. Just when she was ready to dismiss him as a crazy man, he surprised her with some unusual insight. And he was so physically expressive that she didn't know exactly how to interpret him. His fleeting kisses and caresses

were at once provocative and impersonal, just his
natural way of reconciling a misunderstanding.

"Look!" He caught her elbow and pulled her to his
side as he gestured enthusiastically toward the view
that opened before them. At their feet, in descending
tiers of stone seats, the amphitheater nestled in a
natural hollow in the side of the mountain. The
"stage" was a semicircular earthen floor, which
would soon be covered over with the foundations of
the set for *Romeo and Juliet*. At the back of this playing area was a wall of spruce trees and mountain
laurel.

From this vantage point over the tops of the trees, a
magnificent panorama of the entire San Francisco
Bay area could be glimpsed. "It reminds me of the
Riviera," Nick commented softly, ruffling her hair
with his breath. In the foreground, the sinuous hills of
Marin—some forested, some bare—undulated down
toward the water. On the left, Rebecca could see the
marina of Sausalito and guess where her own summer
houseboat home was moored. In the far distance, over
the Golden Gate Bridge, San Francisco floated in the
brilliant sunlight like some magical, white fairy-tale
city on the edge of the Pacific.

From there, one's eye followed the long graceful
Bay Bridge east over the water to Oakland, Berkeley
and the hills beyond. Rising out of the shimmering bay
were two contrasting islands: the bleak fortress of
Alcatraz and the lovely forested Angel Island. Sea
gulls circled and rode the air currents. And the boats
were everywhere, their white sails dotting the bay like
daisies.

"Aren't you chilled?" Nick inquired as his fingers
ran lightly down one of her bare arms before clasping
it at the wrist. "There's a wind up here today." He
swung her around in front of him as his eyes swept
over the frail peach-colored sundress with its thin
spaghetti straps. She shivered under his gaze. "See,
you *are* cold," he admonished. "What am I going to

do with you? I can't have my lead actress coming down with a cold or laryngitis." He sucked in his breath and raised the palm of his hand playfully as if he were going to strike her for her oversight. But when he cupped her cheek, his touch was warm and gentle.

"No, really, I'm fine." She shrugged, flushing under the attention. "Really I am."

"Look at you." He smiled, raising her chin to observe the new color in her cheeks. "You've got a glass head, do you know that? I can see everything that's going on in it."

She pulled away from him, startled. "You cannot," she insisted.

"Of course I can." His eyes twinkled with humor and delight. "You're so transparent and so vulnerable that you immediately register everything you feel. A man has only to look at you and you blush like a rose."

"That's not true," she protested, blushing an even deeper shade of crimson. She turned her back on him and looked out over the amphitheater in a vain attempt to conceal her distress.

"Becca!" He spoke with a rich dark laughter in his voice. "I don't say this to upset you. On the contrary, it's a very good quality in an actress. Especially a Juliet." He had taken off his jacket and was slipping it around her shoulders. When she inhaled, she once again caught the special earthy scent of him, which subtly permeated the tweedy material. She took off the coat and handed it back to him.

"No!" He patiently but insistently persuaded her to put her arms into the sleeves while he buttoned up the front. "I want you healthy for that rehearsal tomorrow morning. I want to hear that voice, clear and strong." Noticing how the sleeves hung comically below her hands, he chuckled, rolled them over into a wide cuff and pushed them up her arms. "There," he said, pausing to adjust the shoulders before he was satisfied. "And you mustn't take it off until I bring you home. That's an order from your director. Now, run down to the stage and let me hear a few lines. I want to check out the acoustics.''

"Terrible man," she whispered as she strode down the stone steps leading to the stage. While Nick's keen power of perception might make him a brilliant director, it also made him a most trying companion. It was no fun having the privacy of one's thoughts continually invaded by his uncanny gaze.

"Perfect," he called from the top row when she had reached the center of the stage. "Give me a line or two. Anything will do."

She took a deep breath and began with the first lines that came into her head.

"My bounty is as boundless as the sea,
My love as deep. The more I give to thee,
The more I have, for both are infinite."

"More voice," he shouted back at her. "I'm losing some words. Your *what* as deep?"

"My *love* as deep," she responded, featuring the word. It was somehow embarrassing, playing these lines to Nick at full volume. She wished Chris were here to partner her and put her at her ease.

"The more you give to *whom*, the more you have?" he demanded.

"The more I give to *thee*," she sang out, summoning up all the vocal support she possessed.

"Well, all right!" he shouted back. "Great!" In a few seconds, he had joined her on the floor of the amphitheater. "This is a big place," he told her. "I'm going to give you some vocal exercises and you must do them first thing every morning. Agreed?"

She nodded. Nick Corelli was probably going to prove to be every bit the taskmaster she had anticipated. "Anything else?" she asked him saucily.

"Yes, as a matter of fact." He gave her a long burning look. "Are you in love with anyone, Rebecca?"

"Why, what does that have to do with anything?" she sputtered. The man was too much. What right had he to ask such a personal question?

"I don't think you are," he decided, studying her intently. "I don't think you understood the lines you just spoke. Not really."

"Don't you worry, Mr. Corelli," she retorted angrily. "By opening night, you will believe every word that comes out of my mouth."

He laughed. "Good. Good. I'm sure I will." Nick shook his head and made a little clucking sound with his tongue. "*Mr.* Corelli...please! You are so touchy. So feisty." He reached out to stroke her hair consolingly, then quickly thought better of it and withdrew his hand. "But your temper is very good in some ways," he affirmed. "If you channel it correctly, you will achieve much.

"For instance, the first time you read for me, I thought you were very sensitive, very responsive. But I didn't know if you had the fire and the drive to play the starring role. I was going to give you the understudy.

"The second time you read, you surprised me. You were bold, adventurous. I could see in you both the vulnerable girl Juliet starts out as and the passionate woman she becomes. And I could also see how much you wanted the role."

"I wanted it very badly," she confessed, disarmed by what he had told her. "I was afraid you had already given it to Evany. She had so much more experience."

"Evany..." Nick mused. "Yes, she was very eager to play the part. But too sophisticated. If I had been looking for a young Cleopatra, I would have cast her." Apparently Evany's charms had not been entirely lost on him. "She's a good actress. I gave her the part of Lady Capulet, your mother."

Rebecca was taken aback. "But she's too young to be my mother!"

Nick disagreed. "Not in this play. Juliet is thirteen

when she marries Romeo. Lady Capulet was also a child bride, making her about twenty-seven at the beginning of the play. I wanted to make a point by having the mother and daughter look more like sisters.''

Rebecca nodded. So, she would be working with the flamboyant Ms Pace after all.

"Come on," Nick told her. "The sun is going down. Let's go back to the car before you do catch cold." He smiled and reached over to turn the collar of his jacket up around her throat.

His mouth was disturbingly close to her own. In her mind's eye, she saw it descend, soft and warm, upon her lips. The taste of him would be dark and lingering; the pressure of his embrace, a ring of fire. The fantasy swept over her in a flash before she knew where it had come from. She gave a little gasp, shocked by the promptings of her imagination.

"What's wrong?" Nick asked. For once, he was seemingly unaware of what she was thinking.

"I was only wondering...you must be cold yourself," she faltered. "Please take back your jacket."

"Nothing doing," he told her with a grin. "I'll be okay. I'm a very warm-blooded animal."

On the drive home, she searched desperately for a safe topic of conversation. "How did Noel manage to lure you all the way to Shakespeare Bay for the summer?" she asked him. "I'd have thought you would be tied up with projects in New York."

He made a face. "Who wants to stay in New York in the summertime? Especially when there's an opportunity to come somewhere as beautiful as this." With a nod of his head, he indicated the view from her window. To their left, the sun was making a technicolor descent below that thin line where the sky met the ocean. All around them the landscape was bathed in the magical shifting light. "Besides," he continued, "Shakespeare Bay has a very good reputation and I'm a great fan of Noel's."

"Yes?" she asked. "How so?"

"I saw Noel's production of *Hamlet* on Broadway when I was fourteen," he told her. "It made such an impression on me that I decided to become a theater director then and there."

"Really?" She was intrigued. "Tell me about it."

"I'll tell you about it over dinner," he promised. "It's a long story."

"Dinner?" She was confused. "What do you mean?"

"We're going to dinner in North Beach," he announced matter of factly. "You are hungry, aren't you? I know I'm ravenous."

"But..." she said, stalling, "how... how do you know I don't already have plans?"

"Do you?" he asked casually. "Well, they couldn't be too important. After all, we've already determined that you're not in love."

"You are the most..." she fumed, searching for the right word.

"Arrogant and presumptuous man you've ever met." He finished the sentence for her with a wink of his eye. "But you'll come anyway, won't you? The restaurant belongs to a friend of my father's and I can assure you that the *cioppino* is out of this world."

Rebecca sat back in her seat and released her breath in a long sigh. She was half-vexed with him and half-charmed by his invitation. And, frankly, a little afraid to spend an evening alone with this very attractive man to whom her senses responded before her mind had given its permission.

"Well, Becca?" he teased, confident of what her answer would be.

"You've just passed the exit to my house," she told him.

"Have I?" he remarked coolly, luxuriously.

"I'm not properly dressed." It was the last argument she could think of.

"It's not a fancy place," he said. "It's a tiny family-

run restaurant. Cozy. Quaint. Great food. Besides,
you have no choice.''

In a scant twenty minutes, they had crossed the
Golden Gate Bridge, made their way over some of the
steepest hills San Francisco had to offer, parked the
car and were comfortably seated at a table in a little
Italian restaurant located in a colorful neighborhood
noted for its little Italian restaurants. ''My father
always used to dine in North Beach whenever he came
to San Francisco,'' Nick told her over the promised
cioppino, a delicious chowder filled with bits of
seafood. ''He was a director of operas and my mother
was a rather well-known soprano in her day. They
both used to work from time to time at the San Francisco Opera House. I remember them bringing me to
this restaurant for the first time when I was about
seven years old.''

Rebecca was fascinated. How very different it all
sounded from her lonely provincial childhood in the
wilds of Mendocino. ''Are you Italian or American?''
she asked him. ''I can never tell. You don't really have
an accent, but you use a lot of Italian words.''

''I have Italian citizenship,'' he explained, ''and a
'green card,' which allows me to work in this country.'' His striking face was illuminated by the candle-
glow, which heightened the hollows beneath his
cheekbones and made his eyes look even more mys-
teriously deep-set beneath his dark brows. He noticed
her studying him and reached over to cover her slender
hand with his own. Once again, a mental image
flashed unbidden into her head. She saw that hand
reach up and cup her face, pulling it gently toward his
own parted lips. Rebecca shook her head as if to rid it
of the unwanted fantasy. She was thankful for the
darkness of the restaurant and settled back into the
shadows, determined to keep her mind on what Nick
was telling her.

''I was born in Italy,'' she heard him saying, ''but,
when I was six years old, we moved to New York

City—because of my parents' careers. I went to a private school there until my mother died when I was fourteen." He spoke matter of factly, betraying little emotion on the subject. "My father had been very dependent on her, and when he lost her, he moved back to Italy and literally buried himself in work. I went with him, but we quarreled a lot and soon I moved out on my own. I grew up very quickly, ran with a very fast social set in Rome and nearly burned myself out until I finally became involved with an experimental theater group there."

He paused and refilled his wineglass and Rebecca's from the bottle of fine dark burgundy the proprietor had given them, compliments of the house. "I was an actor, a carpenter, a stagehand, a lighting designer, before I finally moved into directing. It was good because I no longer felt I was in competition with my father, and besides, the theater appeals to me more than opera. I had found my niche. Eventually I had some successes. I began to get offers from other cities, other countries, and here I am." He smiled. "You have my life in a nutshell."

"I have your *career* in a nutshell," she corrected him.

"Touché," he said, then chuckled, toasting her with his glass. "You're very quick. And you're right. Most of my adult life has been centered around my career."

"You've never married?" she heard herself asking. It was a most personal question but her curiosity—and the unaccustomed headiness of the wine—had got the best of her.

"No." He took a swallow, then pensively circled the rim of the glass with his finger. "I've known a number of remarkable women, but I've never been inclined to marry. And I don't think I ever will."

"No. . ." she murmured, echoing him.

"I'm married to the theater," he told her. "It's a damned nomadic life at best. It's murder on relationships."

"But your parents?"

"It was difficult for them in more ways than I care to enumerate."

"You don't have a very high opinion of the institution, I gather?" she said lightly, finishing off her glass.

"For some people, I'm sure it's the only answer. But for me.... If you want to know the truth, I think marriage is a response to societal pressures, born out of personal insecurity. Someone who feels like half a person meets someone else who feels like half a person and they marry, have children, accumulate property and drive each other crazy for the next fifty years. No thanks." He rocked back in his chair and surveyed the shocked expression on her face with some amusement. "Poor Rebecca. She's horrified," he teased.

"I can't say it's the most romantic definition of marriage I've ever heard," she conceded.

"Ah, you young girls. Always hungry for romance." The mocking smile now danced upon his lips. "Well, I'm sure someday you'll meet a boy who's just as romantic as you are and you'll be the one in a thousand who goes on to a happy ending." He glanced at his watch. "Look, do you want some coffee or shall we be on our way?"

"Coffee will only keep me awake," she told him. "And we both have a rehearsal in the morning."

"Spoken like a pro," he congratulated her. In a few minutes he had paid the check, bid an extravagant goodbye to the proprietor of the restaurant, and they were on their way. The ride home was silent except for the classical piano music Nick had found on the radio. As they crossed the bridge, the night sky was illuminated by the diamondlike sparkling skylines of the cities and towns that bordered the bay. Rebecca stared out the window, feeling somewhat stung by Nick's words. It was silly, she told herself. They barely knew each other. Why should she allow his opinions to carry any weight with her?

"Are you angry with me?" he asked when they had reached the parking lot at Gate Five. "Did I curdle your food for you?"

"No," she said, accepting the hand he offered to help her out of the car. "I just don't happen to agree with you."

"Of course you don't," he responded cheerfully. "Besides, as Juliet, you've got to believe that love is worth everything, even dying for...." They were walking along the pier toward the houseboat, their footsteps echoing hollowly against the wooden planks. "Say, this is quite an interesting place you've found for yourself," he remarked, pausing to admire some of the other barges. A cool wind had sprung up off the bay. From somewhere came the sound of wind chimes tinkling faintly in the breeze.

"Yes," she agreed. "It's a wonderful zoo."

"Look at that." He caught her elbow and pointed at a large sign nailed to a weathered-looking houseboat anchored off by itself in the dark water. Keep off the Grass, the sign said.

Rebecca laughed. Nick did, too. For a moment their eyes met, all sense of estrangement falling suddenly away. "Well..." she said at last.

"Well..." he repeated, his eyes warm and crinkling with rakish good humor.

"Thanks for a terrific dinner," she told him hurriedly. "And here, I'm giving you back your jacket."

"No," he insisted. "Keep it. I don't want you to get chilled."

"I won't get chilled in the minute it will take me to unlock the door to my houseboat." She unbuttoned the coat and slipped out of it. "Besides, I don't want to be responsible. It looks expensive and I have this cat."

He took the jacket reluctantly. "Look at you. You're already covered in goose bumps," he admonished as he pulled her to him and rubbed his hands rapidly up and down her arms. Catching her fingers between his palms, he quickly massaged the cold out of them, then blew against them with the heat of his breath.

She freed one hand and pushed against his chest, laughing, disconcerted. "Let me go...really...I'm fine...." She was suddenly giddy with the sheer nearness of him and longed to break away before he could notice.

It was too late. His hand slid up along her bare shoulder and held her fast. She gasped faintly as his mouth found hers in a warm lingering kiss. Then he released her, tracing his forefinger across the curve of her lower lip. "Don't look so shocked, *bambina*," he told her in a low whisper. "You've been wanting me to do that all evening. Don't deny it."

She stared back at him, speechless with outrage.

"Now quick, run inside," he commanded. "I want you to get up at seven, eat a good breakfast, do some voice exercises and be at the theater by a quarter to ten. Understand?" He kissed the tips of his fingers in a farewell gesture. "Ciao."

CHAPTER THREE

NICK WAS ALL BUSINESS the next morning when she saw him in the crowded rehearsal room at Shakespeare Bay. Looking every inch the director in a dark-blue tailored shirt and slacks with a cream-colored sweater knotted casually around his shoulders, he greeted her politely and showed her to a seat at a long table in the center of the room. This was the first time the entire cast had assembled to read through the play and the air fairly hummed with a sense of expectancy. Some actors embraced one another like long-lost friends. Others were helping themselves to the coffee and doughnuts provided for the occasion. In a corner, one dedicated-looking fellow was standing on his head.

"Nicky!" Evany's husky voice cut through the surrounding chatter. "I hope I haven't kept you waiting! I've had a simply ghastly time getting here!" All eyes were on her as she swept breathlessly into the room and greeted Nick with a kiss on the cheek. Even in this company, the woman knew how to take center stage.

"No, Evany," Nick told her with an amused smile. "As you can see, we haven't begun—"

"Thank God!" she breathed, tossing off a rainbow-colored shawl to reveal a most fetching outfit underneath. The sleeveless, emerald-green knit dress clung to her figure, saucily emphasizing the full bosom and long shapely legs. "I rode over with Fred here," she continued, indicating the mutely infatuated young man at her side. "And I told him, I said, 'Fred, if I'm late to that rehearsal, I will absolutely slit my throat.'"

"Evany," Nick replied sardonically, "under no circumstances may you slit your throat without first obtaining my express permission. I'm much too busy to waste time replacing you."

She threw back her head and roared with laughter. "You're so funny," she gasped, holding on to his arm as if for support. "You have the most evil sense of humor, Nick Corelli."

Nick only smiled and led her to the chair beside Rebecca. "I believe you've met Rebecca Yates," he told her.

"Well, of course," Evany chirruped brightly. "Noel's little goddaughter. Congratulations."

Nick's attention was pulled away by the arrival of his producer and he disappeared into the crowd, leaving the two women alone. Evany seated herself next to Rebecca and flashed her most ingratiating smile. "It must be awfully nice having a relative in the business," she mused. "You're lucky Noel was around to put in a good word for you during the auditions... twist Nick's arm a little."

Rebecca was stunned by the insinuation. "I don't think anyone twists Nick's arm," she responded coolly.

Her tone was not lost on Evany, who regarded her with a faint look of surprise and then promptly changed the subject. "He is something, isn't he?" she whispered conspiratorially to Rebecca, as her smoky eyes followed Nick across the room. "The most delicious man I have seen in many a moon."

"I hear he's a very fine director," Rebecca replied noncommittally. "Did you know he's been nominated for a Tony?"

"Yes," Evany replied, then pressed, "But don't you think he's just marvelously sexy to boot?"

"Well, I really haven't....." Rebecca was at a loss. "I mean...."

"Not your type?" Evany concluded with a note of pleasure in her voice. "Good. Because he is definitely mine."

Rebecca was much relieved when Chris Matheson came over to join them at the table. "Hello, Becca. Big day, huh?" He grinned as he took off his jacket and hung it over the empty chair to her right. "Hi, Evany."

"Hi, honey," Evany responded absently with a little toss of her henna-red curls. Her attention was still fixed on Nick, who was deep in conference with Noel on the other side of the room.

"You're looking awfully pretty, Juliet," Chris announced as he sat down beside Rebecca. "Do you know all your lines?"

Rebecca laughed aloud for the first time that morning and thanked heaven that she had at least one unequivocal friend to take the pressure off the rehearsal. "Are you kidding?" she asked him ruefully. "Have you seen all the stuff we have to learn?"

"That's what you get for being the star," he told her airily. "Lots and lots and lots of lines."

"Can we have a little quiet, please?" Nick was calling the rehearsal to order. "Could everyone come and take a seat?"

It was a fascinating spectrum of people who hurried to fill the remaining places around the long script-laden table. The majority of the faces were young and eager, but mixed in among them were a few veteran character actors, looking as if they had been through it all a thousand times before but were nonetheless pleased to be embarking upon this new venture. Chris leaned over, putting his arm around the back of Rebecca's chair and pointed out those he recognized. "Sasha Constantine," he whispered reverently, indicating a heavyset, middle-aged woman across the table. "And the young black actor next to her is Gabe Daniels...." Rebecca nodded, but her attention had wandered elsewhere. For a moment she thought she saw Nick observing the two of them out of the corner of his eye. But she couldn't be sure.

"We are here," Nick began, capturing the attention

of the group with his deep, resonant voice, "to bring
to life one of the greatest love stories in the history of
the theater...."

NICK CONTINUED TO MAINTAIN a professional distance
for the remainder of the week. Rebecca saw him only
in rehearsals, where he was demanding but patient,
observing her every move in that intense detached
manner of his she found so unsettling. It was as if she
had ceased to have any individual identity in his eyes
and had become, instead, only the character named
Juliet. The evening in North Beach, with all its cozy
familiarity, might never have happened.

Perhaps it was just as well, Rebecca told herself. At
home at night, when she was curled up in bed with
Samcat and her script, her thoughts sometimes
strayed to that brief disturbing kiss. It was best forgotten. It had obviously been nothing more than a mo-
mentary impulse of his. And if she were only a little
more experienced in these matters, she might be able
to put it out of mind as easily as he had. Besides, the
work was the important thing now.

And there was always plenty of work. Rebecca
began to put in long hours outside of rehearsals studying her scenes, memorizing lines, poring over the notes
Nick had given her. She was determined to do her best.
Evany's insinuation that she had been cast because of
her relationship with Noel continued to nag at her. It
wasn't true, of course. But how many others might
secretly be thinking the very same thing? The only way
she could rise above such speculation would be to
succeed—totally—in the part.

The hard work appeared to pay off at rehearsal the
following Wednesday morning. She made her way
through a particularly long and difficult section
without blowing a single line. Chris, who was still carrying the script in one hand, congratulated her warmly
as did several other cast members. Afterward, aglow
with newfound confidence, she waltzed into the green-

room to check on the afternoon schedule. Act 3, scene 5, she noted; it was a love scene between Chris and her.

The room was empty. Everyone had apparently hurried off to make the most of the lunch break between rehearsals. In fact, the whole beehive of a building was quiet—except for two muffled voices involved in a discussion inside Noel's office. "And then there's Rebecca," she heard someone remark.

Instinctively she hesitated outside the door and listened to what was being said about her.

"She's like a young colt." It was Nick's voice. "She's lively and she's eager and she doesn't quite know what to do with herself. She's very rough around the edges. Of course, I'm used to working with much more polished, experienced actresses...."

His words sent a faint chill through her. It was certainly not the sort of thing she wanted to hear, but still she could not tear herself away. She stepped a little closer to the crack in the door and held her breath.

Noel was speaking now, but she couldn't catch what he was saying. His voice was too subdued. Then Nick laughed and spoke again. "Well, Evany is chomping at the bit to play the role, you know. And she certainly does have the experience...."

Rebecca's heart froze in her chest. Were they considering replacing her? With Evany? But it wasn't fair. She had worked so hard. Her face was instantly aflame and she could feel her eyes beginning to water. "Eager... like a colt...." Apparently he had noted the enthusiasm with which she approached the work, but it was not enough to satisfy him. He thought her only quaint. He had made fun of her to Noel.

"Well, I'll be off now," she heard Nick saying as he took a step toward the door. Catching her breath, Rebecca turned and fled soundlessly down the empty corridor. Her heart was pounding in her ears. Not only had she overheard this most damning of criticism but she had almost been caught eavesdropping. She ducked into the rehearsal hall and leaned heavily against the cool brick wall.

What if she were fired? What if the role were taken away from her? The thoughts echoed through her head in a feverish litany. What if she were fired? Nick Corelli had no heart at all. Treating her like a joke.

Suddenly the door opened and a hand turned on the light switch. Nick walked into the room and picked up a script from a chair in the corner. Then, catching sight of her flattened against the wall, he paused and regarded her with a quizzical expression. "Hello," he said with a smile. "What are you doing here?"

"Nothing," she replied, looking away into space.

"Nothing?" He chuckled. "You look like something out of *Macbeth*. You look like you've just seen a ghost or witnessed the murder of your children."

"Excuse me," she responded curtly, moving toward the door.

"Becca...." He caught her by the hand. "Just a minute."

She turned to face him with a baleful look in her eyes.

"What is wrong with you?" he demanded, a frown darkening his handsome face. She was silent. He shook her hand playfully. "Come on. I'll take you to lunch. I think you're working too hard."

She snatched her hand out of his grip. "No thanks," she flared. "Just leave me alone, you... you...." Then, before he could respond, she strode out of the room, slamming the door behind her.

To her surprise, Chris was waiting for her outside the building. Taking note of her emotional state, he persuaded her to go with him to a little waterfront restaurant not too far from the theater and tell him what was bothering her.

"I'm afraid they're going to fire me," she confessed after she had shamefacedly related the whole eavesdropping incident. "What am I going to do, Chris?"

"I don't know," he told her frankly. "Are you sure you heard him correctly?"

"Yes!" she insisted, unconsciously shredding the paper napkin in her lap.

"Well, let's hope it's not as bad as it sounded."

"It was awful."

"Sweetheart, it's your first job." He spoke soothingly. "You're a little insecure. You don't know where you stand. Maybe you should have a talk with Nick. Now I wasn't there and I don't know what's going on in his head, but I think you're doing fine. I've been in the business sixteen of my twenty-three years and I do have some savvy. . . ."

The waitress had come for their order, a pretty, frizzy-haired woman attired in Chinese lounging pajamas. "A dozen oysters on the half shell," Chris told her, glancing over the menu, "and a chef's salad."

Rebecca watched him with a certain admiration. Although his open face and fair tousled hair gave him the innocent appearance of a Renaissance choirboy, there was something poised and worldly in his manner, as if he truly had been an adult all of his life. And beneath the worldliness was some vulnerability, some inner frailty that surfaced from time to time in his eyes. How very different Chris was from Nick Corelli: Nick—that fiend—always burning like Lucifer at the edge of her thoughts.

"Stop frowning, Becca, and tell us what you'd like for lunch." Chris reached over and shook her arm, rousing her from her reverie.

"Oh, I can't think," she murmured, looking blankly at the menu. "I'm not really hungry."

"A bowl of clam chowder for the lady," Chris told the waitress, "and do you have any sourdough bread?" The frizzy-haired woman nodded and departed with their order. "Look at this place," Chris joked, in an effort to cheer her up. "It's so California-hip I can hardly stand it. Ferns everywhere and the waitress looks as if she just rolled out of bed."

He was right. Plants trailed from the ceiling and sprouted from nooks in the curvilinear wood paneling that surrounded each table like the hollowed-out trunk of a tree. Ceiling fans circled lazily. Over the entrance to the room hung a weathered statue of a mermaid, probably rescued from the bow of some old ship. It might all be a bit much for Chris's taste, but she thought it was fun.

"Why, look who's here!" a familiar voice exclaimed. Beneath the hovering mermaid, Evany was making a noisy entrance down the wide oaken staircase that led into the dining area. Her arm was linked chummily through Nick's, and her eyes sparkled with excitement and high spirits. Rebecca moaned faintly and ducked her head. These were the last two people she wanted to encounter at this moment. Nick paused briefly and looked out over the restaurant to see whom Evany had meant. He had slipped a fawn-colored, suede jacket on over the burgundy sweater teamed with gray slacks he'd been wearing earlier at rehearsal, and looked for all the world like some figure out of a European fashion magazine; only his once-broken nose and restless masculinity balanced out the perfect elegance of his appearance. He spotted Rebecca at last and nodded, an indecipherable smile playing faintly at the corners of his mouth.

Evany was dragging him over to their table. "Look, it's Becca and Chris—together again!" She laughed. "Oh, Nicky, don't they make a perfect couple? Like two cherubs in a painting by, whatsisname, Botticelli?"

"Hello, Chris," Nick greeted him amiably. "How's the food here? Is there anything you can recommend?" His glance traveled lazily over Rebecca, but he purposely failed to say hello.

"All of the seafood's pretty good," Chris offered. "Except for the prawns. They're frozen. Would you care to join us?" But before he could move over, Rebecca gave him an impulsive kick under the table.

Chris winced and flashed her a sidelong look of surprise.

Nick chuckled. "Thanks, but I think not. I seem to have a bad effect upon Miss Yates's digestion. Besides, here comes your waitress with your lunch. I'll see you back at the theater." He smiled nonchalantly and escorted Evany over to a table by the window. Outside, rain had begun to fall, turning the blue water to gray. All across the bay, sailboats were heading back to the safety of the harbor.

Rebecca felt her spirits darken with the weather. What if Nick had brought Evany here to offer her the role of Juliet? Perhaps he had reconsidered his earlier evaluation of the actress as "too sophisticated" and now preferred her expertise to Rebecca's inexperience.

"Cut it out," Chris told her firmly. He sampled one of his oysters and then pointed to the steaming bowl of chowder in front of her. "Eat."

"Cut what out?" she asked him.

He reached over and tapped her forehead with his finger. "All that worrying," he insisted. "You're not going to be fired. You're going back to rehearsal this afternoon and be brilliant. Why do you let a few careless words from Nick upset you so?" He shook his head and chuckled. "Are you infatuated with him or something?"

"Don't be silly," she responded hotly. "I don't even like the man." Her gaze wandered over to the table by the window. Nick was rocking back in his chair, laughing heartily at something Evany had said. Evany smiled, fished a cigarette from her purse and leaned seductively forward with her elbows on the table. As Nick struck a match for her, she gently encircled his wrist with her left hand and lingeringly accepted the favor. "He may be...a good director," Rebecca concluded raggedly, "but, personally, I find him unbearable."

"Yes, ma'am." Chris decided to drop the subject. "Whatever you say."

Rebecca suddenly felt very foolish. She sampled her chowder and cast quickly around for another topic of conversation. "Will your family be coming up for the opening?" she asked a little too brightly. "After watching your show for so many years, I almost feel as if I know them—your mother and father and your sisters. . . ."

Chris shrugged, his boyish face clouding with a look of melancholy that she had seen before. "I don't know," he said. "Maybe. My family isn't really together anymore. They're scattered all over the place."

"Oh," Rebecca murmured, sorry she had asked the question. "I didn't know. . . ."

"Of course you didn't. Most of America remembers us as the folks-next-door." He gave a little laugh and looked down at his hands.

"I noticed the other day that you asked me all about my life and said very little about yourself," she began quietly. "I'm sorry. I don't mean to pry. You certainly don't have to tell me anything."

"No...no...." He shook his head. "It's just that...so many people stop me and ask me questions because they remember 'Our House' and they feel as if they know me. And some of those questions are tough to answer. You see, after the show ended, life became very difficult for my family." He toyed absently with an empty oyster shell on his plate. "It was as if we had been blessed for a long time, and then all of a sudden the roof caved in. My sister Molly was drowned in a river-rafting trip in Colorado, which really devastated all of us. . . ."

"Oh, yes. . . . How awful. I vaguely remember something in the papers. . . ." It was coming back to her now.

"But I think Mia was hit the hardest of all because she was her twin." His face had taken on an odd transparent quality as if he were made of glass. "She withdrew from me and from my folks. She ran away from home a couple of times, started getting into trouble. Needless to say, all this put a lot of strain on my parents' marriage. They eventually divorced. And, of course, the newspapers were there, publicizing each new development.''

"I can see why you feel so strongly about your privacy.''

"That's it." He nodded. "Everyone goes through hard times but not everyone does it publicly. Finally, I took some of the money I'd earned and left the country. I went to drama school in London and studied the classics. Eventually I began to find some identity for myself as an individual, not as some famous member of a 'tragic' family. I still want to be a good actor. But I don't care to be a famous one." He took a bite of his salad and smiled at last. "I guess that's why I find it a little hard to relate to this sunny picture of the way we all were on 'Our House.' It seems as if it happened to someone else...."

"I don't want to sound presumptuous," Rebecca said, "but I think I understand at least part of what you feel."

"I know you do." Chris reached for her hand. "Maybe that's why I feel so close to you. Besides, you remind me a little bit of my sister...."

Rebecca leaned over and kissed him on the cheek, feeling strangely protective toward him. She knew what it was to lose a loved one, but she was also suddenly aware of her own inner resources. It was as if she were somehow stronger than Chris. There was something very fragile about him, really.

"Well, I certainly didn't mean to get morose on you," he apologized as he reached for the check. "The past is past and the present is delightful."

"You didn't get morose on me." She smiled, wiping her hands on her napkin. "You got a little salad dressing on me, but I forgive you."

"That," he said with a laugh, kissing her back, "is the worst joke I've heard all day."

Across the room, Nick looked up from his conversation with Evany and cast them a brief comprehensive glance.

THE AFTERNOON REHEARSAL was progressing fitfully. Rebecca's uncertainty about her status in the company was affecting her performance. She felt constrained, ill at ease. She stumbled over lines and went through the love scene in a hesitant halfhearted manner. Try though she might, she could not seem to recover her former enthusiasm.

At last Nick lost his patience. "Look," he told her emphatically, "I don't know what's wrong with you this afternoon and I don't care. When you come to a rehearsal, you leave all your problems outside the door, understand?"

She nodded, thankful that there was no one else present but Chris and herself.

"A theater is a very special space," he continued, raking one hand through his dark hair in exasperation. "It's where we come to create. You must honor that space. You must come to rehearsal one hundred percent ready to work. Nothing less will do."

"I'm sorry," she murmured.

"I'm not interested in 'sorry.'" He took off his jacket, threw it carelessly over a chair and pushed up the sleeves of his sweater. "Spare me your 'sorries.' Just tell me, do you understand this scene?"

"I think so." Rattled though she was, she couldn't help but note the passion with which he approached the work. His black eyes now sparkled angrily beneath his brows, and his whole frame was animated with feeling.

"I don't think you do," he countered. "This scene takes place the morning after their wedding. They've slept together for the first time. Juliet has become a woman overnight. She wakes up in the arms of her beloved."

She nodded in agreement. "Yes. . . ."

"Well, I didn't see any of that in your performance," Nick continued. "You played the whole scene as if you were having a polite tea party with a total stranger."

Rebecca flushed.

"Well, that's better," he grinned sardonically, noting the color in her cheeks. "That's a little more like it. You should be flushed, drowsy. What else? What else might you be feeling for this man you've just given yourself to—your lover...your lord... your husband...your friend?"

Rebecca turned an even deeper shade of crimson. "I don't—"

"Don't tell me you don't know. I won't accept it." Nick was adamant. "You're an actress. It's your job to come up with the answers. You must find every character within yourself. You must think, 'What would I be like in that situation? What would I do?' "

She looked down at the floor. How could she tell him she had never been in that situation?

Nick sighed. "Look, maybe you touch his face when you wake up. Maybe you kiss him. I don't care what you do. I just want to feel that this is your husband. Now, let's try it again."

She never knew where she found the courage, but somehow, beneath the confusion and the embarrassment and the desire to prove something to Nick, it was there. She delivered her lines to Chris with an intimacy she had never truly experienced in life, touching him, caressing his face, following his every move with a loving glance. At the end of the scene, she threw herself into his arms and kissed him lingeringly.

When it was over, Chris appeared dazed and a little goofy with delight. Nick regarded her with an odd veiled look and then scribbled a few notes onto a clipboard he held in his lap. He was silent for a moment, as if he'd disappeared inside himself, as if he were somehow taken aback by what she'd done. *"Bene,"* he told her at last. "Good. This is a play of passion. If it's not performed with that intensity, it just doesn't work.''

"Nick," Chris interrupted, looking at his watch, "I'm five minutes late for a costume fitting. What should I do?"

"Go on." Nick handed him a page of notes. "I promised Maggie I'd let her have you at five. Read this over and we'll talk in the morning."

"Thanks." Chris grabbed his jacket and his script and hurried off to his appointment.

Rebecca sat down on the floor of the rehearsal hall and pretended to look at her script. She was suddenly a little embarrassed by her audacity. She felt as if she had exposed herself in some awful way by playing the scene so fully. But wasn't that exactly what Nick had been pushing her to do? To play the scene fully? She didn't know. She shielded her eyes with her hand and struggled to gain control of the host of emotions warring within her. Today Nick was driving harder than ever. Why? Just to prove his point about her limitations? Just to create an opportunity to fire her?

"You look enormously confused," he said, walking over to where she sat. "You look as if you have a big black thunderstorm hovering over your head."

"That's a pretty accurate description," she agreed, eyeing him distrustfully.

"I don't get it!" The impatience was back in his voice. "I thought we just solved the scene. I thought we just made some progress. Was I wrong?"

"No...."

"No?" he demanded angrily. "Then what is it? Look, I would like to know what's going on with you. You've been impossible all day long. I ask you to lunch, you're hostile. We come back to rehearsal, you're hostile. We make a major breakthrough with this scene, again you're hostile. I've had it with you, Rebecca. Now either you tell me what this is all about or—"

"Or what?" she flared, scrambling up off the floor

to confront him. "Or you'll fire me? If that's what you've already decided, then why don't you say so!"

"Wait a minute." He was baffled. "Who said anything about firing you?"

"You did!" she insisted hotly.

"When?"

"This morning...in Noel's office...." The words were out of her mouth before she could stop them.

"What?" He looked at her in disbelief. Then a big grin broke across his face. "And where were you at the time?"

"I was in the greenroom," she replied, chin held high. "I couldn't help hearing."

He uttered a rich throaty chuckle. "Eavesdropping!"

"I was not."

"I thought I heard someone out there!" A gleam had come into his eye as if he had just put two and two together and arrived at the right answer. "So that's why you were hiding in the rehearsal hall. That's why you nearly bit my head off when I asked you to lunch!" He pressed one hand to his forehead and began to laugh helplessly. He looked at her and started to speak but could not find his voice. Finally he had to sit down in a chair and catch his breath. "Such a little spitfire—"

It was fuel to the flame. "I'm not a joke, Nick!" she replied, incensed. "Regardless of what you may think."

"Of course you're not a joke." He smiled. "But you are one of the funniest people I've ever met—always flying off the handle about something." His eyes swept over her face and then he shook his head and laughed again. "One minute you're just heartbreakingly sweet and demure and trembly, and the next you're a raging five-alarm fire."

"Well, I'm glad you're amused," she responded sarcastically. "I hope you laugh yourself to death. Pardon me if I don't stick around for the funeral."

She picked up her bag and her shawl and headed for the door.

"Just a minute, Becca," he called, his voice suddenly serious again. "This discussion isn't over yet. And for that matter, this rehearsal isn't over yet, either."

But she was gone, out the door, down the hall and out the front entrance of the building. The rain was still falling and a thin fog had rolled in off the sea. She threw the shawl over her head and hugged the bag to her chest. Today she had neither bike nor car to see her home. If she started walking now, she just might make it back to the houseboat before dark.

She had gone about six blocks when Nick pulled up beside her in the Porsche. "Get in the car, Rebecca," he called from the window. "Now!" His voice was dark with anger.

She continued walking as if she hadn't heard him. He pulled up a little ahead of her, stopped the car and got out. "Go away," she told him. "Leave me alone."

"Damn it," he muttered, grabbing her by the arm. "Will you get in the car before we both drown?"

The rain was falling hard now, drenching them both. She started to protest, but he was pushing her around the car and into the passenger seat. Then he slammed the door behind her, hurried through the downpour to the driver's side and slid in behind the wheel. "I ought to fire you," he said as he made his way through the early-evening traffic. "Don't you ever walk out of a rehearsal again. You can do anything you like on your own time, but don't ever walk out of a rehearsal until I say it's over."

She turned her head, looking away from him to the window at her right and sneezed.

"And don't you dare catch a cold!" he commanded, a tiny muscle quivering in his jaw. "Little idiot... running out into the rain." He reached over and turned on the heater. "I hired you to play this part," he told her emphatically. "I intend to see that you do

1. How do you rate _____
   (Please print book TITLE)

   1.6 ☐ excellent   .4 ☐ good   .2 ☐ not so good
   .5 ☐ very good   .3 ☐ fair   .1 ☐ poor

2. How likely are you to purchase another book:
   in this *series* ?   by this *author* ?
   2.1 ☐ definitely would purchase   3.1 ☐ definitely would purchase
   .2 ☐ probably would puchase   .2 ☐ probably would puchase
   .3 ☐ probably would not purchase   .3 ☐ probably would not purchase
   .4 ☐ definitely would not purchase   .4 ☐ definitely would not purchase

   G123

3. How does this book compare with similar books you usually read?
   4.1 ☐ far better than others   .2 ☐ better than others   .3 ☐ about the
   .4 ☐ not as good   .5 ☐ definitely not as good   same

4. Please check the statements you feel best describe this book.
   5. ☐ Easy to read   6. ☐ Too much violence/anger
   7. ☐ Realistic conflict   8. ☐ Wholesome/not too sexy
   9. ☐ Too sexy   10. ☐ Interesting characters
   11. ☐ Original plot   12. ☐ Especially romantic
   13. ☐ Not enough humor   14. ☐ Difficult to read
   15. ☐ Didn't like the subject   16. ☐ Good humor in story
   17. ☐ Too predictable   18. ☐ Not enough description of setting
   19. ☐ Believable characters   20. ☐ Fast paced
   21. ☐ Couldn't put the book down   22. ☐ Heroine too juvenile/weak/silly
   23. ☐ Made me feel good   24. ☐ Too many foreign/unfamiliar words
   25. ☐ Hero too dominating   26. ☐ Too wholesome/not sexy enough
   27. ☐ Not enough romance   28. ☐ Liked the setting
   29. ☐ Ideal hero   30. ☐ Heroine too independent
   31. ☐ Slow moving   32. ☐ Unrealistic conflict
   33. ☐ Not enough suspense   34. ☐ Sensuous/not too sexy
   35. ☐ Liked the subject   36. ☐ Too much description of setting

5. What *most* prompted you to buy this book?
   37. ☐ Read others in series   38. ☐ Title   39. ☐ Cover art
   40. ☐ Friend's recommendation 41. ☐ Author   42. ☐ In-store display
   43. ☐ TV, radio or magazine ad 44. ☐ Price   45. ☐ Story outline
   46. ☐ Ad inside other books   47. ☐ Other _____ (please specify)

6. Please indicate how many romance paperbacks you read in a month.
   48.1 ☐ 1 to 4   .2 ☐ 5 to 10   .3 ☐ 11 to 15   .4 ☐ more than 15

7. Please indicate your sex and age group.
   49.1 ☐ Male   50.1 ☐ under 15   .3 ☐ 25-34   .5 ☐ 50-64
   .2 ☐ Female   .2 ☐ 15-24   .4 ☐ 35-49   .6 ☐ 65 or older

8. Have you any additional comments about this book?
   _____ (51)
   _____ (53)

Thank you for completing and returning this questionnaire.

Printed in USA

NAME _____
ADDRESS _____
(Please Print)
CITY _____
ZIP CODE _____

BUSINESS REPLY MAIL

FIRST CLASS   PERMIT NO. 70   TEMPE, AZ.

POSTAGE WILL BE PAID BY ADDRESSEE

NATIONAL READER SURVEYS

2504 West Southern Avenue
Tempe, AZ   85282

play this part. I expect you to stay healthy, work hard and stop indulging in wild fantasies about being fired. Believe me, if I decided to fire you, you'd be first to know. I'm a very direct person.''

She looked over at him in wonderment. "Then you're not going to replace me?"

"If you hadn't been so quick to fly off the handle, if you'd had the good sense to refrain from eavesdropping, or if you'd come right into Noel's office and confronted me on the spot, you'd know that I never had any intention of firing you. I merely said that although you don't have the experience and polish of many actresses who've been at it a good deal longer, your freshness and your naiveté might very well work for you in this part. Of course, you'll have to work very hard on the verse, but I'll help you. And you're going to have to adopt a more mature attitude and stop creating trouble for yourself." He paused for a moment as he spotted the entrance to Gate Five Road and turned into it. "So can we agree on that? Can we call a little peace?"

She sighed, feeling as if a great burden had just been lifted from her shoulders. "Nick, I feel very foolish. I don't know what to say...."

"Say you'll continue to make progress and be astoundingly good by opening night."

She laughed. "I'll do my best. I really will. Oh, Nick, I've been a great baboon. I do hope you can forgive my unprofessional behavior. Chalk it up to temporary insanity."

He parked the car, switched off the engine and turned to regard her with a wry smile. "It's an emotional business. Sometimes life spills over into the play and sometimes the play spills over into life. I guess everyone is entitled to one outburst per show."

"One? That means I've already exhausted my quota?"

"That's right." He chuckled. "Santa Maria, look at you, you're soaked to the skin. What am I going to do with you, Becca?'' He leaned over and lifted the shawl from her head. Her dark hair clung damply to her face and cascaded down her back in a thick tangle. He made a little clucking sound and attempted to towel it dry with a corner of the shawl.

She laughed. ''You're all wet yourself.'' It was true. Water glistened in his hair and beard, stood out in beads across the fuzzy surface of his sweater. A tiny rivelet made its way down the canal of the half-moon scar next to his eye. She impulsively reached out and touched it with her fingers. ''How did you get the scar?'' she asked, childlike with curiosity.

A rueful smile flickered over his face. ''A long time ago—'' he nodded, as if in deference to the memory ''—a lady threw a vase at me. . . .''

''I see. And did you deserve it?''

He grinned. ''Probably.'' His eyes caught hers for a moment and they both laughed softly.

''Well,'' Rebecca murmured, suddenly aware of the smallness of the space in which she found herself enclosed with Nick. ''I'd better go in.''

''Wait a few minutes,'' Nick advised. ''It's pouring out there. Wait until it slacks off.'' The rain was pounding across the roof of the Porsche. She shivered and rubbed her hands together for warmth. ''Oh, I'm sorry. I'll turn the heat back on,'' he offered, switching on the ignition. ''It'll fog up the windows—not that it matters.''

''Thanks.''

''And get rid of that soggy old thing.'' He reached over and tossed her shawl into the back seat. She shivered again. Out in the bay, a lone foghorn sounded hauntingly in the growing darkness. Nick ran his finger along the embroidered yoke of the Mexican peasant blouse she had chosen to wear with a soft cotton skirt for rehearsal. ''You know, you always wear these lovely fragile little dresses, with no warmth to them at all. . . .''

''It was sunny when I left the house this morning.''

She shifted slightly in her seat, conscious of how the gauzy material clung damply to her.

Nick smiled and fished a wet strand of hair off of her neck. "Oops," he said and laughed, "there's a couple of raindrops I missed."

"Where?" she asked, flustered.

"There," he whispered as he leaned over and softly kissed the hollow of her throat. At the touch of his lips, she felt a subtle warmth begin to permeate every cell of her body. She raised her hand and pushed gently against his shoulder.

"Nick...."

His mouth grazed the side of her neck and hovered warmly over her ear. "Yes?" he murmured, cupping her cheek with his hand, turning her head toward him.

"Nick, don't...." She became aware of that sweet earthy scent of him, and her heart pounded against her breastbone.

"Why not?" He seemed genuinely amused, his dark eyes lazy and soft. "Why ever not?" He wound his fingers loosely into her hair and inclined his head to kiss her.

"Because," she whispered, turning her face away, "it frightens me...."

His fingers tightened, gathering up the hair at her nape. "Don't be coy with me, Rebecca," he told her with a twinkle in his eye. "It doesn't frighten you half as much as it excites you." He held her gaze with that penetrating look of his, as if he were seeing deep down into the well of her soul and finding at the bottom no objection at all. She was mesmerized. With his free hand, he delicately traced the full curve of her lips. "You're trembling," he said softly. "Shall I kiss you now?"

"Yes." She mouthed the word soundlessly. With tantalizing slowness he leaned forward and brushed his lips back and forth across her own, hesitating for a moment at each corner of her mouth. She moaned faintly, drunk with the heady enveloping presence of him as she felt her body arch involuntarily toward him. Still he did not kiss her but held himself a millimeter away, palpable and suspended. What was he waiting for? Everything in her now ached for him. At last she could stand it no longer and, wrapping her arms around his neck, she pulled him close and drank the kiss from his mouth like one too parched with thirst to wait. She felt him sigh.

Now he took the lead again, powerfully, inexorably. The pressure of his hand upon her forced her lips to part, and he invaded her mouth hungrily with his tongue. The taste of him was the bittersweet taste of the stems of wild flowers she had once sucked on as a child, lying lost in daydreams on her back in a meadow. She felt as if she were falling down a long dark tunnel through time. Nick's hand slid along her throat and pressed against the top of her chest, just below her collarbone, where he could feel the heavy rise and fall of her breath.

With fingertips now sensitized and feeling swollen from the throbbing of her pulse, she ran her hands through the silky thickness of his hair, tracing the fine contours of his skull. From somewhere, she heard the foghorn-moan again but could not be sure if the sound had originated outside or within herself or Nick. At last he relinquished her mouth and followed the arch of her hairline, bestowing small kisses on each temple. "Beautiful eyes," he said, tracing the rim of her lids with his breath. "Witch eyes...."

"Nick," she murmured drowsily, glancing over his shoulder toward the window of the car, "I think it's stopped raining."

"Good." He grinned, pulling back to gaze at her. Her hair was appealingly disheveled and his eyes were bright with feeling. "Now you can invite me inside. This is all very sweet—" he took her hand and buried a kiss in its palm "—but a sports car is not the most comfortable of places."

She hesitated and lowered her eyes. Ask him in? That would surely prove a most dangerous invitation. She was neither ready to encounter him nor confident she could resist.

"Nick, I can't..." she began hesitantly. "I can't invite you in. This is...too much. It's too fast. Too much too fast."

"What is, *cara*? What? Isn't it obvious that we are highly excited by each other?"

"I just can't...." Her voice trailed off and she looked away in desperation.

"Ah..." he mused. "I think I see now. I've noticed you've become very chummy with your co-star of late. Apparently Romeo is not a case of 'too much, too fast.'"

"Chris and I aren't...." Rebecca was instantly incensed.

"No? And what were you discussing so ardently over lunch. Let me guess. Shakespeare?"

"It's none of your business."

"You're right." His voice suddenly was that of the cool detached professional she had known at the theater. "But one piece of advice, my friend. It's not a very good idea to get involved with your leading man. I don't want you two falling in love and then breaking up right before opening night and spoiling the work we've done. Business is business and pleasure is pleasure and they are best kept separate."

"Oh. I see." Rebecca felt her temper starting to rise. "And just what was that you were introducing me to a few minutes ago? Business or pleasure?"

"Touché." He shrugged. "You're right again. It was probably a very poor idea on my part. It won't happen again." He reached into the back seat for her shawl and wrapped it around her shoulders. "I just hadn't counted on your being such a potent little witch, Becca. Now hurry home and don't tempt me anymore."

She gathered up her bag and reached for the door

handle in a fit of blind fury. "You may be. . .a great director," she sputtered, "but, personally, you are really the most presumptuous—"

"Save it," he commanded. "You have a costume fitting at one o'clock tomorrow. Don't be late."

"Don't worry," she snapped, scrambling out of the car.

"And Becca," he said just before she could slam the door.

"What?"

"I meant what I said." He grinned, and then suddenly looked strangely serious. "You really are a potent little witch, and I—" He stopped.

Her eyes held his for a moment, then utterly confused, she closed the door and walked quickly down the deserted pier, not once looking back.

CHAPTER FOUR

"DON'T MOVE!" Maggie Byrne warned her. "Don't even breathe!"

Rebecca remained obediently frozen as the costumer made a few quick strategic marks along the front paneling on the bodice of her gown.

"I'm sorry to put you through such a long fitting," Maggie continued in a hushed voice as she concentrated on the task at hand, "but this material was *very* expensive, my dear—I'm not even going to tell Noel how much it cost or he'll have my head on a platter. Anyway, I bought the last bolt of it and I can't afford to make any mistakes."

Rebecca glanced at her reflection in the long mirror. It was a stunning dress, the most lavish of all Juliet's costumes, designed to be worn to the ball that climaxes the first act of the play. The material was a deep rose brocade, which set off her coloring to best advantage. The neckline was sweetly decolleté, exposing her neck and shoulders and just enough cleavage to be alluring without seeming out-of-character. A generous, floor-length skirt fell from the empire waist, but the crowning glory of it all was the sleeves. They were slashed, in keeping with high Renaissance fashion. Maggie had cut long slits in the material, pulled the delicate, cream-colored lining through so that it could be seen and then laced the slits together again with satin ribbons at three-inch intervals. As if that were not enough, she had sewn dozens of seed pearls over the shoulders and around the wrists, which caught the light and cast an iridescent shimmer.

"Can I breathe now?" Rebecca murmured through clenched teeth, scarcely daring to move her lips.

"Oh, child, yes!" Maggie exclaimed, as she stood up at last and dusted off her knees. "You can breathe all you want. I'm finished. But don't take it off yet. Nick will be coming over in just a minute to take a look."

"Nick?" Rebecca was surprised. She had not expected to see him at all that day and had been glad of it, too. The previous evening's encounter had left her feeling most self-conscious. "I thought he was rehearsing the fencing sequence," she told Maggie. "You know, the death of Mercutio and all that jazz."

"He is," Maggie affirmed. "But he's coming over during the break specifically to check out this costume. He's a very unusual director, you know. He takes an interest in every aspect of the production—the costumes, the lights, the set. Lots of directors are content just to let me do my thing; they look at my sketches and then they don't see the costumes again until dress rehearsal. But not Nick. Oh, no. He's already mastered all of our jobs. He could build the set; he could probably even sew up this costume if he had the time."

"No!" Rebecca couldn't see Nick Corelli wielding needle and thread.

"Oh, yes!" Maggie insisted. "I've worked with him before. I was assistant costumer on the very first show he directed in New York eight years ago. He wasn't the celebrity he is now, but he was still just as much of a perfectionist. Some people think he's a real pain in the neck, but I've gotta respect him for it." She perched herself on top of a high stool and ran her fingers through her short curly hair. To Rebecca, Maggie always seemed as if she had just flown in on the evening breeze like Peter Pan. This slender pixieish woman had proved to be the owner of the houseboat next door, but because of the difference in their schedules she and Rebecca seldom saw each other. Maggie and her staff frequently worked late into the night in an effort to finish the large number of complicated costumes needed for the production.

Maggie took a sip from the ever-present cup of coffee that kept her going, and then giggled as she remembered something else. "Once Nick decided he didn't like the cut of a particular dress the leading woman had to wear. So he stuffed it into a briefcase when the head honcho of the costume department wasn't looking, carried it home, took it apart and then put it back together again overnight. He said he just didn't trust anyone else to carry out his idea." She smiled. "I think he trusts me though. Pretty much. As much as that grouchy old Italian bear trusts anyone—"

"Who's a grouchy old Italian bear?" a voice demanded from the stairwell leading up to the costume department. Nick's head surfaced above the railing and regarded Maggie with a ferocious look. Rebecca caught her breath.

"You are!" Maggie retorted playfully. "You can be the meanest old bear around, but I like you anyway. Now, come on over here and look at this costume. I've had Rebecca on her feet for an hour and a half and she's ready to keel over."

Nick grinned and walked over to kiss Maggie on the cheek. The two were obviously old friends. "Ooph!" Maggie shook her head in mock disgust. "When are you going to shave that beard, Corelli? People will think you don't have a chin."

"I don't," he confessed.

"He does!" Maggie told Rebecca as she reached over to adjust the neckline of the gown. "He has a very nice chin. Now—" she turned her attention back to Nick "—what do you think? Is this gorgeous or what?"

Nick stepped back and cast an appraising look at the picture Rebecca made. His eyes swept absently over her face and he failed to say hello. His whole attention was on the dress. *"Bellisima!"* he congratulated Maggie. "You've really surpassed yourself this time, Ms Byrne."

"It's the best thing I've ever done," Maggie agreed without a trace of vanity. "And Rebecca looks smashing in it, doesn't she?"

Nick shrugged. "She looks okay."

"Smashing!" Maggie repeated. "Look, Nicky, if there's anything you want changed, speak now or forever hold your peace. By the time you get back from New York, this costume will be finished. When are you leaving?"

"Tomorrow night. The awards are on Sunday and I'll be back on Monday. That way I'll only miss one rehearsal."

"You're flying back for the Tonys?" Rebecca spoke up at last. In her absorption with this play, she'd almost forgotten that Nick had another, much-nominated show running in New York.

He nodded. "I'd just as soon skip it. But my manager thinks I should go."

"Of course you should," Maggie encouraged. "We'll all be rooting for you."

"Thanks." He gave her a wry smile. "But the whole thing's a lot of nonsense, if you ask me. I'd rather be working than sitting around at some stuffy awards ceremony."

Maggie laughed. "You're a workaholic. It'll be good for you to go."

"Right. . . right. . ." he muttered with a noticeable lack of enthusiasm. "Now, what concerns me about this dress is. . . can she dance in it?"

"I don't see why not," Maggie said.

"Come here, Rebecca." He reached for her hand, giving her his full attention for the first time since he had entered the room. "Let's go through a couple of the steps and see what happens. This lovely creation is no good to us if you can't move in it." He swept her out into the center of the room.

The dress now had a subtle but magical effect upon

her, imbuing her with a new sense of size and regality. It demanded things of her. It demanded that she live up to its grandeur. There was no way one could shy away and blend into the woodwork in such a dress. She drew herself up to her full height and looked Nick Corelli squarely in the eye.

"Good," he said. "Daughter of the House of Capulet." He put his arm around her waist and led her through the opening steps of the dance she had been learning. She followed him effortlessly, aware of the flow of electricity between them. His palm burned like a brand through the layers of fabric into the flesh at her side. "How is it?" he asked her quietly. "Does the train get in your way?"

"No," she replied in a husky voice. "I can manage it." The room had begun to recede and she was aware only of his presence. She could not say for certain whether Maggie was still there or not.

"Good." He swung her out in front of him. "Now curtsey." She complied, dropping to one knee, still holding on to his hand. It was as if they were both slipping backward to some other place in time. How long had she known him? Many lifetimes? Had he always been her lord?

He gently raised her back to her feet. "And around...two...three...four..." he said, counting the beats aloud. She circled him, the luxurious train of the gown rustling in her wake. "And back to me," he commanded, catching her by the waist with both hands and lifting her off the ground as her hands pressed down upon his shoulders. She could feel two bright spots of color burning in her cheeks as she slid at last down the front of his body and found herself gazing full into his face. Nick hesitated for a moment and then released her.

"Well," he told Maggie. "Everything seems to be fine. But just to be safe, I'd cut another three inches off that train. I don't want her tripping over it."

"You're the boss," Maggie replied with a wise look

in her eye. "Rebecca dances very well, don't you think?"

"She's not bad," he admitted gruffly. "But she needs a lot of work. They all need a lot of work. Starting tomorrow morning, Gabe Daniels is going to be teaching a nine o'clock dance class for everyone involved in the ball scene." He turned back to Rebecca with that taskmaster gleam in his eye. All the actors had come to recognize it; it usually meant that he was about to have them working twice as hard as before. "That means you, Chris, Evany, Roger, Holly, Milton, Bibi . . . just about everyone but Sasha. You're all too slow on your feet. The class will help you not only with the ball scene but with the pace of the entire show. The way you guys are playing it now, it's going to be a five-hour opus. We can't expect the audience to sit there more than two and a half hours!" His eyes sparkled blackly as if he were angry with her, angry with all of them. He continued on with his tirade. "So, that's nine o'clock tomorrow morning and every weekday morning until this production opens. And if I hear that you or anyone else is skipping Gabe's class, heads are going to roll!"

"Nick!" Rebecca interrupted, aware that her own temper was starting to build. "I'll go to the class. All right? Give me a break. Don't threaten me about missing class when the class hasn't even begun!"

"Give you a break," he muttered. "Have you been doing those voice exercises I gave you?"

"Yes *sir*!" she snapped.

"Do you know your lines for act 5?"

"Just about!"

"Well, I want you off book by the time I get back from New York! We've got a lot of work ahead of us. *Capisce?* Understand?" He turned to gather up his jacket and his script and headed for the staircase. "I'm late for rehearsal," he told them. "Keep up the good work, Maggie."

When he had gone, Rebecca turned to Maggie with

a look of shock written over her face. "What is he so wound up about?" she asked her friend. "Is he suffering from brain snappage?"

Maggie regarded her with an impish smile. "I think he really likes you."

SHE DID NOT SEE NICK AGAIN before he left for New York. He had spent the time before his departure working and reworking a long fight sequence that involved most of the young men in the cast but none of the women. She had gone to Gabe's dance class Friday morning and then settled back to life on the houseboat, overwhelmed with the unaccustomed leisure. After working nonstop for the past couple of weeks, she hardly knew what to do with herself.

She soon discovered all those basics of life—the laundry, grocery shopping, housecleaning—that had been totally neglected of late. Saturday and Sunday were spent cleaning and polishing the houseboat and stocking the empty refrigerator. Samcat followed her happily from room to room as though covetous of her company. The tiger cat was now heavily pregnant.

By Sunday evening Rebecca was lonesome for a fellow human being and decided to invite Maggie over for supper. Although the two women were neighbors, neither had found the time to visit the other's boat. Rebecca located the costumer in her office at the theater where she was working through the afternoon of her day off. "I make a pretty good shrimp curry," Rebecca told her. "What do you say?"

"Bless you, child!" Maggie exclaimed. "I'm so tired I'd probably have just come home and had a couple of spoonfuls of peanut butter. I'd much rather sample your curry."

"You're on. How's seven o'clock?"

"Do you have a television over there?"

"Yes." Rebecca was puzzled. "Why?"

Maggie enlightened her. "The Tonys! We have to watch Nick on the Tonys!"

"Oh... well, yes, there's a TV."

"Terrific. I'll see you around seven."

"I TRULY HOPE he does win," Rebecca told Samcat later as she chopped up the condiments for the curry. "Whatever else you may say about him, he is a wonderful director. I'm learning so much...." Samcat was oblivious to this account of Nick's virtues. The animal studied the five little bowls of raisins, peanuts, shredded coconut, chutney and crumbled cooked egg, and then made a tentative swat with her paw in the direction of the last.

Rebecca lifted the bowl out of the cat's reach. "Not for you, my friend!" she admonished. The doorbell rang and she hurried to answer it, carrying the dish with her. "Come on into the kitchen," was her breathless greeting to Maggie. "I can't leave Perry's cat alone with our dinner."

"Hello, Samcat! Hello, old puss!" Maggie called out merrily from the living room. "I love this boat!" She sighed as she took off her windbreaker and hung it on a peg beside the door. "Have you heard any news from Perry?"

"He's in France now," Rebecca told her. "My brother had a letter from him last week."

Maggie wandered into the kitchen and sat down at the circular wooden cable-spool table by the window. "Is your brother a tall lanky fellow? Brown hair? Spooky eyes like yours?"

Rebecca laughed. "That's him. Adam. His name's Adam."

"I've seen him once or twice with Perry. But I could never manage to engage him in a conversation."

"He's very shy."

"He's cute," Maggie commented with her pixie smile. "Is he married?"

"No," Rebecca replied, amused as always by her friend's directness. "He's a cranky old bachelor."

"How old?"

"Thirty-five."

"Hmm." Maggie mulled this over. "Same as me."

"You've never been married?" Rebecca inquired, turning off the gas under the pot of curry and reaching for a couple of plates.

"Nope." Maggie shrugged. "Too busy with my career. Too driven. Too much of a workaholic. Nick and I have that in common. But I made a new resolution this year. I'm going to put some time into Maggie . . . as well as Maggie's career. Problem is, I don't know just how to begin."

"Well, I'd be glad to introduce you to my brother," Rebecca offered. "But I warn you he's very hard to get to know."

"He seems like a nice man."

"He's a wonderful man."

"Well, a good man is hard to find," Maggie drawled.

"Just how long have you been at this career of yours?" Rebecca ladled a large serving of the curried shrimp onto a bed of rice and served it to Maggie. "You know how to eat this, don't you? Take whichever condiments appeal to you and sprinkle them over the top."

"You're an angel for doing this." Maggie thanked her as she leaned forward to inhale the aromas rising from the steaming plate. There was a comically blissful look upon her face. "I've been creating costumes for about ten years now. Nick's production of *Six Characters in Search of an Author* was one of my first professional gigs."

"You two go back a long way. . . ." Rebecca filled her own plate from the pot and crossed to join Maggie at the table.

"Do we ever!" Maggie sampled the curry and gave a little moan of delight. "*Six Characters* was the first show Nick did after he broke up with Francesca Cini," she told Rebecca. "He needed a friend in those days, and we became rather close. Not that I've ever had an affair with him, mind you." Maggie laughed. "I'm sure one of the reasons Nick and I have remained friends is because we have absolutely no romantic interest in each other."

"Who's Francesca Cini?" Rebecca asked. She was fascinated by this unexpected insight into the enigmatic Mr. Corelli's past.

"You've never heard of Francesca Cini?" Maggie exclaimed. "My dear, where have you been all your life?"

"Mendocino."

"Right. Mendocino." Maggie shook her head and chuckled. "Francesca Cini was—and still is—one of the protean figures in European theater. She founded one of the major theater companies in Rome. She discovered and nurtured a lot of the actors you now see starring in Italian movies. She's quite a dame. She found Nick Corelli when he was a nineteen-year-old misfit running around with the café society crowd. He acted for her for several years. I think he played Romeo as a matter of fact. But eventually he switched and became her assistant director. And her lover."

Rebecca choked on a bite of curry and had to wash it down with a large glass of water. "Really?" she asked, dabbing at the corners of her eyes with a napkin.

"Oh, yes," Maggie assured her. "Francesca was a good many years older, but she knew talent when she saw it. They collaborated on a number of projects that were quite successful and attracted a lot of attention. Offstage, their relationship was very stormy. Their fights were legendary among theater folk."

"She threw a vase at him." Rebecca remembered Nick's explanation about the scar next to his eye.

"Did she?" Maggie asked. "Do you know this story already?"

"No." Rebecca shook her head. "Just something Nick said once in passing."

"Well, I don't doubt it," Maggie agreed. "I only

met the woman once, but she was a dynamo, let me tell you. Anyway, by the time Nick was in his midtwenties, he was becoming his own man. The power struggle between them was just too fierce. Eventually the relationship blew up like Mount Vesuvius and Nick came to New York to direct *Six Characters*.''

''Was Francesca content to let him go?''

''No.'' Maggie took a bite of her curry and then continued. ''She followed him to New York. But Nick refused to see her. As far as he was concerned, the thing was finished. I think Francesca had hurt him very badly. Sometimes I rather blame her for spoiling something in my friend Nicky.''

''What do you mean?''

''Well....'' Maggie sighed and spent a moment searching for words. ''Francesca Cini is an extremely dominant woman. Nick's mother was similar. I think, after the two of them, he felt as if he couldn't have an ongoing relationship with a woman without sacrificing his manhood. I've watched him go out with a lot of different women—actresses, ballerinas, career girls, all of them bright, all of them attractive. But he keeps his heart locked away.'' She shrugged. ''I like him. I'd like to see him find someone he can trust and open up all that tenderness and warmth I know he has inside.''

''I think,'' Rebecca suggested, ''that if we want to see the awards, we'd better take our plates into the living room and turn on the television.''

Maggie glanced at her watch. ''Yikes! You're right. The show's half over by now. But that's okay. They won't hand out Best Director until the end.''

Rebecca placed Perry's little portable set on a table in the corner of the room, and the two of them settled down on the sofa with their half-finished dinners in their laps to watch the remainder of the ceremony. *The Taming of the Shrew* won for Best Supporting Actor, lost for Best Set Design and tied for Best Costumes. Rebecca found her mind wandering back over some of the information Maggie had shared with her. Perhaps Nick Corelli was not quite the fiend she sometimes imagined him to be. Perhaps he truly was a good man in search of a good woman. She closed her eyes and recalled the rapturous sensation of his mouth on hers and shivered. His effect on her was undeniable.

All of a sudden Maggie was shaking her arm. "You can't drift off to sleep now! Wake up. Here it comes!"

Rebecca sat up, her heart pounding in her chest. "I'm so nervous for him," she confessed. "I feel as if it's a member of my family. . . or my child. . . or something."

"I know." Maggie reached for her hand and squeezed it. "Me, too."

"The nominees for Best Director are—" one of Broadway's luminaries was reading out the names "—and Nick Corelli for *The Taming of the Shrew*. And the winner is. . . ."

Maggie and Rebecca clutched each other and held their breath.

"Nick Corelli for *The Taming of the Shrew*!"

Maggie cheered. Rebecca felt herself flush with happiness. The camera panned to Nick, resplendent in full formal dress, as he accepted a congratulatory kiss from his companion before sprinting up the aisle to receive his award.

"*What*," Maggie asked in a flat, little voice, "is Evany Pace doing in New York?"

Rebecca had recognized her, too. Evany, looking absolutely radiant in a low-cut white evening gown, was obviously Nick's date for the occasion.

"What is he doing with that hussy?" Maggie demanded. "How did she contrive to get him to take her to the Tonys?"

"Maybe she didn't do anything," Rebecca offered grimly. "Maybe he wanted her to go."

"Give me a break," Maggie groaned. "Evany Pace is looking for a ticket to ride. She's afraid to strike out and try to make it in the big time all by herself, and she thinks Nick is her ticket."

Rebecca felt sick at heart. She didn't know whether or not Maggie's assessment of the situation was correct. All she knew was Nick had taken Evany with him to the biggest event in the theater world, and that could hardly indicate indifference on his part.

"Well, I must say, I'm disappointed," Maggie fumed. "I would certainly have thought Nick would see right through her."

"Apparently not." Rebecca reached to turn off the set.

"Wait...wait." Maggie stopped her. "Hussy or not, we have to listen to his acceptance speech."

"...thank all the people who have shared their talent with me," Nick was saying. He looked marvelously charismatic in his tux, his hair just a trifle too long and hence very romantic. *Just imperfect enough to be more than perfect,* Rebecca thought ruefully. "I thank the theater for blessing me with the opportunity to share that which I consider best in me," he continued. "And I thank the powers-that-be for bringing me to this moment in time."

"Well, that was nice," Maggie said after Nick made his exit. "For someone who didn't want to go, he made a very nice acceptance speech. He's still a prince in my book. I think we should have a party for him when he gets back." She rose reluctantly and looked about for her windbreaker. "I'm off, my dear. Thanks so much for the dinner."

"You're welcome, Maggie," Rebecca told her. "Anytime."

"I'll fix that hussy," Maggie muttered, pausing at the door. "I'll take all her costumes in an extra two inches." Then she laughed and saluted Rebecca in a farewell gesture. "A party's a good idea, don't you think? And why don't you ask that elusive brother of yours."

MAGGIE KEPT HER WORD. By Monday evening, she and Noel had arranged a whackily charming party in Nick's honor on the mountainside grounds adjacent to the amphitheater. A local Greek restaurant had catered a lavish buffet. A xylophone player and a trio of mimes in whiteface had been hired to furnish the entertainment. Everyone associated with Shakespeare Bay had been hastily invited.

As the sun made its descent into the Pacific, the guests began to arrive in carload after carload. Rebecca had phoned Adam that morning and he had seemed pleased at the opportunity to drive down from Mendocino and check up on her. He stood beside her now, looking unusually spruced up in a newly ironed plaid shirt and his favorite cowboy hat.

Rebecca, feeling somewhat ill at ease at the thought of seeing Nick again, had also spent considerable time on her own appearance. The better she looked, she reasoned, the easier it would be to appear lighthearted and carefree when she congratulated Nick on his award. Sometimes grooming could be a very effective camouflage for insecurity.

For the occasion she had chosen a full calf-length skirt worn over burnished leather boots, a soft romantic blouse and a bright shawl. Her hair hung down around her shoulders in loose dark ringlets, and she looked for all the world like a saucy Gypsy dancer. "Where's your tambourine?" Adam kidded her.

"Where's your pony?" she joshed back.

They were soon joined at the buffet by Maggie—in a dress instead of her usual windbreaker and jeans— and Gabe Daniels, the talented young black actor who played the crucial role of Mercutio and also doubled as choreographer. Rebecca made the introductions, and Maggie quickly spirited Adam away by asking ever so sweetly if he would help her hang some paper lanterns she had decided to put up at the last minute. Rebecca giggled. Adam prided himself on being a handyman; there was nothing he loved more than to be of service. It was his Achilles' heel.

"Have you seen our guest of honor?" Gabe asked

Rebecca as he helped himself to the stuffed grape leaves.

"I don't think he's here yet," Rebecca told him breezily. She was determined to get through the evening without allowing any past, present or future action of Nick Corelli's to affect her state of mind.

"Hey! Yonder he comes...." Gabe's face lit up with delight. He and Nick had been working closely together, staging the dance and the fencing sequences, and the two had become fast friends. "My man!" Gabe called, beckoning to Nick to join them.

Nick was making his way through a crowd of well-wishers. He looked tired but handsome in a collarless white shirt, a bulky-knit peasant cardigan and a pair of jeans. And on his arm, the inevitable Evany Pace.

"Evany Pacemaker!" Gabe greeted her. "You fox! I saw you on the awards, sitting there all sleek and sly like the young fox you are!"

"Wasn't it exciting?" Evany gushed. "I went crazy when they called out Nick's name. I was so happy I almost went up on stage with him."

"Congratulations, Nick," Rebecca told him brightly when he had disentangled himself from yet another well-wisher and joined them at last. "I'm very happy for you." Well, that's done, she told herself.

He picked up her hand, kissed the back and held on to it for a long moment. "Thank you, Becca. How are you?"

She struggled to sound gay. "Wonderful. And you?"

"Jet lagged. Glad to be back."

"Don't let him fool you." Evany laughed. "He's elated. He's kissing the hand of every woman in sight."

"Would you care for something to eat?" Rebecca asked him evenly. "Look at this fabulous spread Maggie's put together on your behalf."

"Thanks," he said. "Just let me say hello to Noel

first.'' Then he disappeared back into the crowd, taking Gabe along with him.

"How about you, Evany?" Rebecca continued in her best hostess manner. "Would you like a couple of grape leaves? A little moussaka?"

"No thanks." Evany sighed. "Nick and I ate just a short while ago. As soon as we got off the plane, nothing would do but we had to go by a restaurant in North Beach and show a friend of Nick's the award. The old fellow was very sentimental and insisted on fixing us one of his specialties. I'm stuffed."

Rebecca's heart sank, but she took a deep breath and held her ground. "So how was New York? I've never been there."

"Never been there! Oh, you sweet thing!" Evany giggled. "It was divine. Of course, it was a whirlwind visit. We went to the awards and then a party afterward. I barely had time to do any shopping, but...." She took off her cape to reveal a daring new ensemble; harem pants and a blouse with a neckline that plunged almost to her waist.

"Very exotic," Rebecca told her truthfully. "It looks good on you."

"Oh, Becca." Evany suddenly embraced her as if she were a very old, very dear friend. "I'm just so happy. I'm so in love. I just have to share this with somebody. Nick is the most wonderful man—he's kind and he's gifted and he makes me feel like I never thought I could feel." Then she released Rebecca, reached into her purse for a handkerchief and dabbed moistly at the corners of her eyes. "Have I spoiled my makeup?" she asked quaveringly.

"No," Rebecca said quietly. "You look fine."

"Thank you," Evany said, then smiled. "I want us to be great friends from now on, Becca. I just admire you so much...."

"Really?" Rebecca's voice was flat, but the other woman didn't seem to notice.

"Oh, yes! I want us to be great friends and share all

our secrets," Evany rhapsodized. "I want you to have a wonderful man who'll treat you as well as Nick treats me. Let's find someone for you. What about Chris? Are you still seeing him? Oh, look, there he is!" She gazed feverishly over the heads of the crowd to where Chris stood talking to Maggie and Adam. "Isn't he the sweetest boy? He looks like he just hatched out of an egg—"

"Excuse me, Evany." Rebecca could stand this no longer. "You just reminded me. I have to talk to Chris about something."

"Have fun, honey!" Evany told her with a knowing look. "I love ya!"

Rebecca made her way through the crowd, looking not for her friends but for a place where she could be alone. She slipped into the darkness of the trees and followed the footpath that led to the amphitheater. The tinkling music from the xylophone and the happy party chatter faded behind her as the noise of her own thoughts swelled within her head. Damn it all and damn her errant heart. Why was it that Nick Corelli held such a subtle power over her? Their personal relationship was virtually nonexistent. What had they shared, after all? A few meaningless kisses. Meaningless to whom? To him obviously! He had taken Evany Pace with him to New York for all the world to see. And worse still, he had taken her to the little café in North Beach, still warm in Rebecca's memory.

The amphitheater opened suddenly before her, quiet and ghostly gray in the moonlight. She sat down on one of the stone steps and drew her shawl around her shoulders. Despite the balminess of the night, she was shivering. Were those kisses meaningless to her, she asked herself. No. No, they weren't. Somehow, by those kisses, he had passed into her heart. He was present in her blood. He was there. She could feel him. She was haunted. She was hooked.

Rebecca raised her head with a sigh and fixed her gaze on a lone cold star sparkling brightly out in space, a million million miles away. Could she make a wish on a star as cold as that? Could she wish for a man whose heart was closed to her?

As if in answer to her thoughts, Nick stepped out of the trees and onto the floor of the amphitheater. The half-finished set rose behind him, eerie as a deserted village. He stood there for a moment, scanning the tiers of stone seats, until he saw her. She held her breath and remained motionless, waiting to see what he would do.

Then he was scaling the massive rock-carved steps, his hands thrust deep into the pockets of his sweater. "Hello," he said at last. "What are you doing up here all by yourself?"

"Too much party," she told him. "I needed a break."

"Ahh," he said, nodding, sitting down beside her.

"What are you doing here?" she echoed challengingly. After all, what right had he to ask for explanations?

"Too much party." There was a smile in his voice. "I needed a break."

They were both silent for a moment.

"Besides," he continued, "I saw you leave and come this way. We didn't really get to talk. And you looked so pretty."

She glanced up at him in surprise. "Thanks." There was an awkward pause. She could think of nothing to say. She felt his gaze, intent upon her, even in the darkness. "Well...I meant what I said. I was truly glad to see you win."

"You were glad."

"Yes, I was."

Nick chuckled.

"Why, don't you believe me?"

"Oh, yes." He reached out and playfully wound one of her curls loosely around his finger. "Thank you for the kind words." His eyes sparkled in the moonlight. "Which I'm sure you mean—in a reserved

Anglo-Saxon sort of way." His voice teased and caressed. "But couldn't I have a hug or something? A nice, expansive, Mediterranean hug would be very acceptable. Under the circumstances."

She sat up straighter and wrapped the shawl a notch tighter. Her eyes had narrowed in suspicion even as her pulse had quickened. What was he up to? What sort of game was this? Hadn't he come to the party with Evany? Hadn't he just spent a long weekend with Evany? Was his head so swollen with his success that he thought he could make a conquest of every woman at the party? Kissing their hands as Evany claimed....

"No," she told him. "No hug."

Nick laughed. "What's the matter, *bambina*? Are you still angry with me about the dance class?"

"No."

"Perhaps you're afraid Mr. Matheson might object?"

"No, I'm not." She rose to her feet. "Excuse me, Nick, I really have to be getting back. I promised Maggie I'd help out."

He threw up his hands in mock surrender. "Okay! I give up! You win! No hugs! No nasty old hugs in this theater!" His tone was so comic she couldn't help but smile. "How about a handshake? Just to show we're still friends?"

Rebecca suddenly felt very foolish. The man had just won a Tony, for heaven's sake. The party was in his honor. She extended her palm and clasped his tentatively. Nick grinned and shook her hand politely. He really was so charming. For one fatal moment a look of longing escaped her. He saw it and pulled her to him.

She pushed against him but he had caught her fast, sweeping her up in his arms, cradling her in his lap. "Your first instinct was correct," he teased. "You shouldn't have trusted me for an instant."

"I thought you said this would never happen again," she gasped angrily, taunting him with the promise he'd made the night he'd driven her home in the rain.

His response was droll, devil-may-care. "Whoops! Maybe I was wrong!" He laughed. "Maybe I missed you, Becca. Maybe I should kiss you!" He was clearly in a wild unpredictably playful mood. "Right here! Right now!" He buried a kiss in her hair. "Wow. Look out. You're liable to be defiled right here on the floor of the amphitheater."

She tried to break free of him but it was all in vain. "You obviously think this is some kind of game, Nick," she sputtered. "But I am not amused."

"Pity," he whispered huskily. "Of course it's a game. All of life is a game. It's a wonderful, terrible, joyful, outrageous game." His arms held her tight against his chest. But his eyes were soft as he burrowed past the tangle of her hair that partially obscured her face and found her lips at last.

The kiss was rough, insistent. She clenched her teeth, determined not to respond. "See what a game you make of it?" he murmured. "You resist. I pursue. It's lovely."

"I don't—" Before she could continue, he had taken possession of her mouth once more. As if in a dream, she felt her own arms rise and wind, snakelike, around his neck.

"Nicky!" A husky female voice sang out from somewhere within the eucalyptus grove. "Nicky, where are you? You know I'm blind as a bat after the sun goes down!" There was a scuffling of leaves and the sound of twigs snapping as Evany made her way toward them in the dark.

Nick paused and lifted his head. "Oh, no," he groaned. "Evany."

Rebecca felt as if someone had just thrown a bucket of water over her head. She sat up and attempted to smooth her disheveled hair. "What's the matter, Corelli?" she heard herself say harshly. "Did you forget who you came with?"

"Shh," he whispered, attempting to gather her back into his arms. "Be quiet. Maybe she'll go away."

Rebecca pulled back and stared at him in disbelief. Much as she might personally dislike Evany Pace, she could not forget what the other woman had told her in confidence. "Nick, you can't just ignore her!"

He sighed wearily. "I'm sorry. I've had enough of Evany Pace to last for quite a while, thank you very much. I'd rather be with you, *cara*. Now come and be quiet and maybe she won't find us." He held her shawl in his arms, still warm with her own imprint.

"I can't believe you!" she said hoarsely. "Do you really think women are so disposable?"

"What are you talking about?"

"I'm talking about the fact that you invited Evany to New York and swept her off her feet. She's fallen head over heels in love with you, in case you haven't noticed. Now you bring her to this party, suddenly decide you've had 'enough' and abandon her for the first woman you run into. It's hardly a compliment to me."

"Your concern is admirable." The mocking tone had come back into his voice and she could see his jaw begin to tighten with displeasure. "But I think Evany can take care of herself."

"Well, I'd prefer to be left out of it! And besides, I don't happen to enjoy having someone force himself on me! Did you ever stop to think that maybe I'm just not attracted to you?"

Nick snorted and shook his head before fixing her with that special penetrating gaze of his. "All right," he said. "Maybe I did force myself on you just now. But not without some cause. I was feeling great and I was glad to see you and I was certain that, underneath your funny standoffishness, you were glad to see me, too. I'll tell you something, *cara mia*. There's a constant invitation coming my way from you, whether you're aware of it or not. It's in your eyes. It's in your body. It's clearly there in the way you respond to me.

So don't think you can get on your high horse and pretend otherwise.''

"Give me back my shawl!" she demanded, haughty
with outrage.

"No!" he fired back. "If you're cold now, it's your
own fault. Go on, shiver just a bit and think about all
this. Think about how you deny your own feelings.
Think about how you lie to yourself and to me. It'll do
you good. Maybe you'll decide my arms aren't such a
bad place to be after all."

"Never!" she insisted, her eyes blazing, her whole
body taunt with anger. "Keep the shawl!"

"Nicky!" Evany's voice rang out again, nearer this
time. "Where are you?"

"Over here!" he called back as he held Rebecca
steadily in his gaze. "Well, what are you waiting for?"
he whispered to her. "Why don't you run away?
That's what you do best, isn't it?"

CHAPTER FIVE

REBECCA LAY ON THE FLOOR of the rehearsal hall, her hair streaming damply about her face, her muscles throbbing, her whole body drenched in perspiration. She could hardly find the strength to move. *Damn Nick Corelli,* she thought to herself for the umpteenth time. *This is all his fault!*

"And one-two-three-four!" counted Gabe Daniels. "Come on, Becca! You're the youngest person in this class. If you can't make it through these exercises, no one can. Don't conk out on us now!"

She gritted her teeth, raised both quivering legs into the air and lowered them again to Gabe's excruciatingly slow count. If Evany could hang in there, if Chris could keep pace, then so could she. She fixed her gaze on a single spot on the ceiling and tried to ignore the pain.

Nick had changed the regulation morning dance class to one o'clock in the afternoon this particular Friday in order to give them all a chance to warm up before he arrived at two for a rehearsal of the grand-ball sequence. Thus twenty young bodies now lay on the floor of the cavernous rehearsal hall, huffing and puffing through Gabe's program to the strains of the *Carmina Burana* set to a disco beat. Rebecca sighed. At this rate she'd be dead before rehearsal ever began.

"Only five more minutes," Chris mouthed from across the floor, flashing five fingers at her to make sure she got the message.

She grimaced and moaned to let him know just how she felt about it all.

At that moment the door of the rehearsal hall creaked open and Nick stepped into the room, looking coolly handsome in pale pleated slacks and crewneck sweater. Not a wrinkle. Not a hair out of place. She hated him more than ever. *"O serpent heart, hid with a flow'ring face."* Her mind danced over a speech from the play. *"Beautiful tyrant! Fiend angelical!"*

He crossed his arms and leaned against the doorframe, smiling at the sight of the steamy mass of humanity flailing away before him.

Gabe was taking the class into a final difficult round of situps. They started flat out on the floor and then arched upward into a V, arms above their heads, legs extended several feet off the ground. It was Rebecca's most despised of all the exercises. She adjusted the kerchief that she had rolled into a band around her head and struggled to catch up with the others. Nick caught her eye and chuckled. She lifted herself into a full extension of the pose and stuck out her tongue at him. He covered his heart with his hand and gasped in mock horror as if she had wounded him terribly. It was the friendliest thing he'd done all week.

Ever since their altercation four days ago, he had kept all communication with her confined to his rehearsal notes. And she, for her part, had studiously avoided running into him on any territory outside of the hall. And yet, conversely, the work had begun to grow by leaps and bounds. It was as if all the wild contrary energy between them was now being channeled into the play. Under his sure and skillful guidance she was blooming as an actress and she knew it.

"Okay, folks," Gabe shouted above the music, capturing their attention. "Take five." A chorus of happy groans greeted his announcement. Rebecca collapsed back onto the floor and closed her eyes in exhaustion, allowing the room and everyone in it to vanish for a moment. She had been working hard since nine that morning. Her lunch hour had been spent in another costume fitting. She wondered where she would ever find the stamina to make it through three more hours.

"Need a hand?" When she looked up, Chris was standing over her, reaching down to help her to her feet.

"Do I ever!" She accepted his help gratefully. Her legs wobbled like two wet stalks of spaghetti. Her hair curled damply around her forehead and stuck to the back of her neck. She felt more like some woebegone orphan than a high-bred young lady of Verona. She wrapped a towel around her shoulders and slipped on a rehearsal skirt over her leotard. "Well, here's your Juliet," she told Chris. "Rank as a wilted cabbage."

"If you can stand to work with me," he said with a grin, "I can stand to work with you."

"It's a deal." She laughed. "Just let me look over my lines."

She had scarcely had time to glance at the text before Nick was calling the rehearsal to order. "Put that script away, Becca," he admonished. "You're supposed to be off book."

"I *am* off book," she retorted, dropping the script directly in front of him on the director's table for emphasis.

"Good." He nodded curtly. "I'm pleased to hear it." Once again he had become the detached taskmaster. He sat and watched without interrupting, while the actors made their way once through the entire scene. He pronounced it fair and then proceeded to break it apart. Starting again from the top, he took them painstakingly, inch by inch, through the action, stopping to work out a nuance here, to enliven another moment there, to suggest some subtext or some revealing bit of business for each character. Rebecca marveled at the vast store of his knowledge, his seemingly endless ability to think on his feet. When it came to his job, Nick Corelli was beyond criticism. The scene began to take on a new dimension, new facets. There was no corner of the stage not filled with life. She felt her adrenaline rise as she responded to the challenge of working with this blazingly gifted man.

Although the hour was late, he coaxed them through the scene a third time, concentrating on the choreography. Nick had conceived the ball in a series of three contrasting dances, interspersed throughout the action. The first was feverishly balletic; the second, comic; the third, slow and lyric as the lovers come together for the first time. Now that he knew his actors were confident with the steps, he pushed them even more, encouraging them to bring their personalities into play, so that the dances were not merely interesting in and of themselves but served to further the storytelling.

"You've all worked very hard," he told them when they were done at last. "I'm quite pleased with what I see. It's coming along nicely. Now go home and get some rest." Then, without any more ado, he packed up his notes and scripts and books into a sachel and was gone.

Rebecca sank into an empty chair, shut her eyes and imagined herself at home in a hot bath, up to her neck in bubbles. At this moment, it seemed like the closest thing to Nirvana. Her bone-deep fatigue was beginning to catch up with her. She looked around dumbly for her script.

It wasn't there.

It wasn't there on the folding director's table where she had left it. "Harry," she called to the stage manager, catching him just as he was about to leave. "Did you pick up my script by mistake?"

"No, honey," he told her. "Sorry."

Puzzled, she turned and glanced around the room. The script wasn't on any of the benches. It wasn't on the floor. "Okay, you guys," she addressed the few remaining actors. "Who's got my script?"

A weary chorus of "not me" greeted her, as her cohorts hurriedly gathered up their paraphernalia, eager to go home.

She pressed her palms to her temples and uttered a deep sigh. Where was it? Was she losing her mind? Was it somewhere in plain view and was she too exhausted to see it? She couldn't very well go home without it. It contained all her notes. And she needed to study them over the weekend.

"Watcha need, sugar?" Gabe asked, noting her distracted state.

"Oh, Gabe," she moaned, "I've lost my script. I put it down on that table before rehearsal and now it's vanished."

Gabe nodded. "Well, I do believe Nick packed up everything on that table and took it with him. If you hurry, you just might catch him before he leaves."

"Thanks!" Rebecca cried, picking up her skirt hem, grabbing her bag and dashing out of the room.

Outside, in front of the theater, she looked around in vain for any sign of the black Porsche. The parking spot it had occupied earlier that morning was empty. "Did you see Nick Corelli drive off?" she asked one of the stagehands as he passed her on the sidewalk.

"Yeah," the man told her. "About three minutes ago. You just missed him."

"Oh, no!" She stamped her foot in exasperation. The stagehand chuckled and continued walking. Rebecca fumbled in her bag for car keys. Luckily, the VW was back in running order, and if she left now she just might overtake Nick before he got home. She certainly hoped so. From what Noel had told her, Nick was renting a house near Stinson Beach, which was something of a trek.

When she was five minutes outside of the Sausalito city limits, it was obvious that he had far too much of a lead on her. The road branched off to the left, following the hilly contours of Mount Tamalpais. Nick had no doubt taken it at his usual lightning speed, but she had no intention of racing after the Porsche. There was little alternative but to drive all the way out to the beach. The sun was just going down as she passed the turnoff to the amphitheater and continued along the dizzying snakelike curves that wound down the west slope toward the sea.

She had to rack her brains to remember the location of the house. It was a vacation retreat belonging to a wealthy friend of Noel's, an elderly San Francisco woman who fancied herself a patron of the arts and had been only too happy to rent it to Nick for the duration of his stay. What was the name of the place? Seawind? Fairwind? Fairseas? In the gathering dark, Rebecca spied a weathered fence with a gate marking the entrance to a private estate. Windsong was the inscription over the gate. Well, it was worth a try.

At the end of the long driveway, the black Porsche confirmed her intuition. The house, a fanciful two-story wooden structure, rose before her. A light from one of the windows threw a welcoming arc over the sandy path that led to a front porch. She parked the VW, got out and marched up to the door, silently praying that he had not brought Evany Pace home with him for the evening. She loathed the thought of interrupting any such tête-à-tête. Rebecca rang the bell and held her breath.

Nick opened the door with a quizzical expression on his face, which intensified when he saw her standing there. "Becca," he murmured before a sardonic smile crooked the corners of his mouth. "Good Lord, you look like a stray cat. Come in."

She glanced sheepishly down at her leotard and sagging rehearsal skirt, at the hem of which a pair of leg warmers drooped about her ankles. Her hair had come unbound, and the windy drive had left it tangled in a wild mass around her shoulders. She pushed it back from her face and launched into an explanation of her visit. "No, thanks," she said rapidly, "I won't stay. I'm sorry to bother you, but I think you picked up my script as you were leaving the theater, and I really need to look at it over the weekend. So if you'll just let me have it, I'll be off."

"Your script?" He frowned. "I don't have it."

"Gabe says you picked it up," she insisted. "Please, I'm very tired. I know you are, too. Just check your sachel and then I'll go home."

"Okay." He nodded. "Okay. Come in and I'll take a look."

"No," she said, "I'll stay here."

"Oh, come on," he growled impatiently. "I'm not going to eat you."

Bristling with the challenge, Rebecca stepped inside the door. Nick shook his head as if he thought her quite ridiculous and tromped off into another room. Rebecca leaned wearily against the doorframe and surveyed the cozy scene before her. The living room of this wonderful house was at once both rustic and elegant. The walls were a natural unfinished wood; the ceilings were beamed and rose to a cathedral height; a fire crackled in the hearth, at the foot of which a luxurious Chinese rug spread out to include twin sofas facing each other across a low table. Cut into the wall that faced the sea was an enormous picture window, bordered in stained glass. She wandered over to it, pressed her hands against the surface and peered out. In the moonlight, she could just see the white crests of the breakers as they rolled into shore.

"Well, you were right," Nick said from behind her. "Here it is."

She started at the sound of his voice, then recovered herself and turned around to face him. He held the battered script out toward her. "Oh, good," she said, reaching to take it. "Thanks."

"I'm sorry you had to drive all this way," he said. "You look beat. Why don't you sit down and have a glass of port before you leave?"

"I am beat," she replied, sensing the pull of her own fatigue even as she spoke. "If I sit down, I may not be able to get up. Thanks, anyway."

Nick shrugged. "Suit yourself," he said, opening the front door for her. "I'll turn on the outside lights so you can see where you're going."

Rebecca cast a fleeting wistful glance at the comfort of the room and then headed resolutely out the door. There was no way she was willing to accept his invitation. Her experience had taught her that she could not trust him. Her own heart whispered that she could not trust herself. Besides, she really was beginning to feel a little woozy. The best thing would be to go home, eat something and relax in the bath. She negotiated the front steps in a kind of stupor, only half aware of Nick watching her from the doorway. Suddenly the night rose up and swallowed her. She stumbled and passed out.

When she came to, she was lying on one of the sofas in front of the fire. Nick was kneeling beside her on the floor, stroking her hair back off her brow with one hand. His eyes were soft; his face full of concern. Everything was silent, save for the distant roar of the surf. She sighed faintly and nestled her cheek against his hand. She had no idea how this moment had come about, but in her groggy state it seemed like paradise.

Nick smiled when he saw her stir. "Hello," he said. "How're you feeling?"

"Fine. How are you?"

He chuckled. "Thank you for inquiring. But I'm not the one who just fainted."

"Who fainted?" she asked, dazed.

"You did," he told her. "When's the last time you had something to eat?"

"Oh—" she rubbed her eyes "—you know. Earlier."

"What did you have for lunch?"

"I didn't have lunch. I had a costume fitting."

He snorted and shook his head. "No good. What'd you have for breakfast?"

"Cup of coffee."

"Just a cup of coffee?"

"'Fraid so." She was too disoriented to lie.

"And last night?"

"Tuna-fish sandwich."

"Becca!" His voice was full of frustration, but he continued to stroke her cheek with the back of his hand. "Actresses must take care of themselves. Actresses must eat well. Actresses must take their vitamins. If you weren't already half-zonked, I'd take you and shake you till your brains rattled."

"Don't be mad," she whispered, wide-eyed as any child.

His anger seemed to melt away when he beheld her expression. "I'm not...mad. I'm just...oh, never mind. Now. You just stay where you are, and I'm going to whip up some dinner, all right?"

"No, Nick...." She raised herself onto her elbows. "I can't stay. I'm a mess. I'm dirty and my muscles are all in knots from Gabe's class and—"

"I give a great massage," he interjected.

"And I'm afraid to be alone with you," she finished, blushing.

He paused and regarded her for a long moment. "You are?" he asked, his eyes crinkling with humor.

"Yes," she told him simply.

"You're afraid I'll take advantage of you in your weakened condition?" he teased.

"No, I just...." She hesitated, not knowing how to talk to him about this.

"You really don't trust me, do you?" he asked. She looked down at her lap, overcome with embarrassment. "Well," he conceded wryly, "maybe you have some cause. Now look, there's no way I'm going to let you out of here until you've had something to eat. But I'll make a deal with you. I won't even look at you sideways unless you make the first move. Fair enough?"

She laughed and nodded her head.

"*Bene!* Good! Now, here's the plan. I'm going to give you a piece of fruit, just to get your blood sugar up. Then you can sit in the hot tub and relax while I make dinner."

"The what?" she asked.

"There's a hot tub out on the deck in back. I turned it on as soon as I got home, so it should be ready. And since you're such a modest young woman, there are some swimsuits and towels and robes in the guest room that Mrs. Windsong—I keep forgetting her name—keeps on hand for visitors. I'm sure you can find whatever you need."

The whole idea was far too tempting for Rebecca to protest. She allowed Nick to show her to the guest room, where he left her alone to poke around in a huge walk-in closet filled with beach paraphernalia of every size and description. She found a tanksuit that looked small enough to fit and, shedding her rehearsal clothes, slipped it on. When she emerged through a sliding glass door onto the deck outside, she saw that he had left a tray of apple and cheese slices for her on a table beside the big wooden vat of a hot tub. She was moved by his thoughtfulness. Perhaps this was the side of Nick Corelli that Maggie Byrne had come to love as a friend.

She popped a slice of apple into her mouth and climbed gingerly into the tub, sighing with pleasure when she discovered just how hot it was. She could almost feel her taut muscles instantly begin to soften and relax as she leaned against the side, allowing her head to drop back in delicious abandonment. Overhead, a waxing moon shone down and a host of stars sparkled like diamonds against the deep black velvet of the night sky. The evening was delightfully cool and miraculously free of fog. At the edge of the deck, a few crickets sang, small tenor voices above the deep baritone roar of the ocean.

She had almost drifted off into some altered state of

consciousness, halfway between dreaming and waking, when Nick appeared in the doorway and announced, "Dinner is served in fifteen minutes," before disappearing back into the house. Rebecca climbed regretfully out of the tub, her skin glowing pink in the night air, and padded barefoot into the guest room. Reluctant to slip back into her grimy leotards, she chose an ankle-length caftan from the closet. If Mrs. "Windsong" were all that wealthy, she probably wouldn't mind, Rebecca concluded. Besides Nick had told her to use whatever she needed. She brushed the tangles from her long dusky hair and pinned it loosely on top of her head, allowing a few wayward tendrils to fall and curl around her ears and neck.

"How do you feel?" Nick asked when she found him at last in the kitchen, carefully tending a panful of clam sauce.

"Like I've died and been resurrected," she replied. "Can I help with anything?"

"No, *signorina*," he replied. "I thought we'd eat by the fire. Go in and help yourself to salad. I'll be with you in a moment."

He had set the table between the two sofas for their meal. There was a bottle of white wine and a delectable antipasto. Over some invisible sound system came the soft strains of jazz piano. Rebecca curled up on one of the sofas and marveled at the abundance that surrounded her. No wonder Nick was willing to make the drive back and forth over the mountain every day. Living well was obviously one of his top priorities.

Soon he emerged from the kitchen carrying two steaming plates of linguini and clam sauce. *"Buon appetito,"* he said, setting one of the plates before her. "Would you care for some wine?"

"Just a little," she said, savoring the aroma of the food she was about to consume. "Nick...."

"Si, signorina?" Here in the privacy of his home he was becoming more Latin by the minute.

She smiled. "Thank you for taking care of me. You're being very kind."

He filled her glass with a small flourish. "It's the least I can do. First I work you to death. Then I walk off with your script and cause you such trouble. This is the least I can do to make my amends."

She cocked her head to one side. Here in the firelight, he looked as gentle and as accessible as she had ever seen him. "Maggie told me you were a nice man," she confided, "but I didn't believe her until now."

He laughed. "You've been talking to Maggie, have you?"

Rebecca took her first bite of the linguini and sighed. It was the best she had ever eaten. "She lives next door," she told him. "We watched the Tonys together."

Nick laughed again. "That Maggie! I adore her. She says exactly what she thinks. She gave me such a bad time about all that."

"What do you mean? She was thrilled when you won."

"She didn't approve of my date. She thought I should have taken someone else."

Rebecca hesitated, suddenly uncomfortable with the turn in the conversation. "Well," she said, "it's your right to take whomever you chose."

"Well, I didn't exactly *want* to take Evany," he confessed. "But it just happened to work out that way." When he saw Rebecca's look of bafflement, he smiled, took a thoughtful sip of wine and continued with his story. "At first, I had planned to go with the leading lady from *Shrew*—Connie Mascolo. She's a friend, and her husband was in Europe on business so we thought we'd go together. Well, a few days before the awards, in a burst of sentimentality, Connie's husband flew home from France in order to accompany her to the grand event. When I boarded the plane in San Francisco, I had no idea what I was going to do. Imagine my surprise when Evany came on board and took the seat next to me."

Rebecca's mouth fell open and she had to fill it quickly with a bite of salad in order not to appear foolish.

Nick chuckled. "She said she was going to see a sick relative who was in the hospital in New York. We got to talking and she carried on and on about the Tonys and how it had always been a dream of hers to go, and somewhere over Ohio, when I'd had a couple of Scotches, I asked her. It had crossed my mind that she was up to something, that she'd somehow found out about my situation and hoped to exploit it, but I really didn't care. I had to appreciate her bravado. I think she's quite a character and I figured, why not? Maybe being seen at the ceremony would help her career. So I asked her."

Rebecca was amazed. It certainly put quite a different light on a number of things. "Did you ever find out the truth of the matter?" she asked.

"Well—" Nick leaned back against the pillows and contemplated her question for a moment "—if she was planning to spend most of her time in a hospital, why did she pack an evening dress? I don't know. I just don't know. And perhaps I'm something less than chivalrous for telling you all of this. Perhaps I should give Evany the benefit of the doubt and keep my mouth shut. I do enjoy her—in limited doses. But I feel she's misrepresented the whole incident to a number of people and that really annoys me. And, besides, I can't have you reluctant to set foot inside my house for fear that I'm some heartless cad who uses and abuses women as if they were— how did you put it?—disposable objects."

"I see." At least...she thought she did. Nick's revelation was astonishing. It was a pinprick to the balloon of assumptions she had blown up about his relationship with Evany. Any unanswered questions she might have had quickly receded to the periphery of her consciousness. "Well," she conceded, "I'm sorry if I called you any names."

"No importante," he said, shrugging. "How was the pasta? Would you like some more?"

"Molto bene." She recalled the phrase for "very good" from her one semester of college Italian. "But no more, please. I couldn't eat another bite. *Grazie.*"

His grin told her he had gotten a real kick out of her attempt to speak his native language. *"Prego."* He responded with the Italian equivalent for "you're welcome." He crossed to the fireplace and added another log. Rebecca was once again aware of the catlike ease that accompanied his every action. There was a lithe grace about the man and a brooding sense of great power held in reserve. Her pulse quickened as he swung around once more to face her, his arms casually folded across his chest. "You're looking a lot better, Becca. You have some color in your cheeks."

"You were right." She smiled. "All I needed was a little food."

"And a long soak in the hot tub," he added. "That's usually the first thing I do when I come home after a rehearsal. After all, this is California. I believe the hot tub is your state symbol."

Rebecca laughed. "It was wonderful. All my bones have turned to cartilage."

"No more knotted muscles?"

"Only a few."

He wandered over and sat on the floor beside her. "Let me see your foot," he commanded.

"Why?" she asked, her curiosity piqued.

"Just let me see it," he urged.

Tentatively, she unwound one bare foot from the cross-legged position she enjoyed on the couch and presented it to him. He took it between his warm hands and held it for a moment. "Such a tiny foot," he remarked. "How do you walk on it? This is a baby's foot." Then with practiced skill he began to massage it, his fingers seeking out the hidden sorenesses and pressing into them, causing her to sigh involuntarily. "Now this is not a sexual advance," he teased. "I know we have a deal. This is pressure-point therapy. There are nerve endings in your feet that connect with every part of your body. Sometimes you can relieve a pain in your back just by pressing the corresponding point in your foot."

"Fascinating," she murmured. While he may not have intended it as a sexual advance, her body was nonetheless responding to it as such. A delicious warmth radiated up from the soles of her feet, making her whole nervous system tingle with pleasure. She swallowed nervously and repressed a sudden urge to reach down and touch his hair. Nick had closed his eyes and his face held a look of rapt concentration, as if he were intuitively sensing his way deep into her bones. When he had finished with the left foot, he returned it to her and then proceeded to repeat his technique on the right. Rebecca felt herself sliding helplessly under his spell and wondered if he had any idea of the effect he was having upon her.

When he had finished, he held her foot in the crook of his arm as if it were some small animal that had fallen asleep there. His eyes were soft and oddly serene when she at last raised her own to meet his gaze. For a moment, neither of them moved. It was as if they were suspended within some invisible globe composed of their own powerfully swirling energies.

Nick was the first to speak. "Come on," he said, gently releasing her foot, making no attempt to take advantage of the moment. "Let's take a little walk on the beach before you leave. Walking in the sand is very good exercise for sore muscles."

"All right," she agreed. "But then I really must be getting home."

"*Naturalmente,*" he conceded as he disappeared into the guest room. When he returned, he was carrying her shawl, the one he had refused to relinquish at the party. "You may want this," he said, draping it around her shoulders. "It can get a little chilly by the water." Then he slipped on a light jacket from a peg by the door before escorting her outside by the way of the back deck. A narrow wooden staircase led down into the sand.

The tide was coming in and had almost reached its zenith as they strolled along the water's edge, side-stepping every now and then to escape an inrushing wave. Nick seemed disinclined to further conversation. He kept pace beside her, whistling to himself, making no attempt to hold her hand or touch her in any way. Or perhaps, she thought, he was no longer as interested as he had once seemed.

Rebecca sighed. The very fact of his apparent indifference coupled with his undeniable magnetism made her long for him all the more. Something inside her had been freshly kindled during that mystifying moment they had shared back in the house. She almost wished now that she could be like Nick, bold and free to do as she pleased. Then, disturbed by her thoughts, she broke into a run along the damp sand, leaving Nick behind.

"Where are you going?" he called after her.

"Just for a short jog," she shouted back, waving her hand in the air. The stars burned high overhead as she ran on and on before coming to rest at last where an outcropping of rock met the swelling tide. Panting for breath, Rebecca held her sides, closed her eyes and dropped down into the dry sand. In the distance she could make out Nick's form moving toward her, cool and unhurried as he had been before she left him. The moonlight glinted off his hair, touched the hollow of his cheek and softly illuminated the strong perfection of his body. He seemed to belong to this timeless landscape, a lone figure balanced between sea and shore.

At last he reached her and sank down beside her on his knees in the sand, hands stuffed into the pockets of his jacket, still whistling the refrain of the song he had begun earlier. It was an Italian folk ballad, as slow and mournful as the music of the tide. She could not help but covet the soft curve of his mouth. His gaze was fixed far away, out where the waves were breaking over the rocks offshore.

A moment passed. Then Nick turned and studied her face in the moonlight, as if he were seeing directly inside her brain. His song faded on his lips. "Yes," he murmured. "Kiss me if that's what you want." A half smile caught at the corners of his mouth. "I can't touch you, Becca, remember? My hands are tied. I'm your frog prince. You can leave me here or you can set me free."

Moved by some power within her she only vaguely comprehended, she reached out one quivering hand and cupped the side of his face. His beard was soft beneath her touch, like the pelt of an animal. Rising to her knees, she inclined her head to one side and kissed him gently on the mouth.

"That wasn't so hard, was it?" he whispered. "Now kiss me the way you really want to."

The air between them was thick with electricity. Like one mesmerized, Rebecca lifted her arms and wound them around his neck. She could feel the heat of him radiating through his clothes. Her own body was half-feverish with excitement. With trembling parted lips, she found the dark cave of his mouth and entered it.

She felt him shudder with pleasure as his hands came up and caught her fast by the hair at the back of her neck. Then his tongue was in her mouth, precious, sweet. She felt as if she could feast upon him for the rest of her life, desiring no other food but this. His fingers now loosened the pins in her hair, causing it to cascade around her, enveloping them both in its dark web. Something inside her chest opened like a flower. She leaned heavily against him.

Then Nick was holding her by the shoulders just

far enough away so that he could see her face. His breathing was as ragged as her own, and she was pleased to see that he, too, had been moved by the kiss. "My God, Becca," he said huskily. "And here I thought you were a little girl. But you're not, are you? You're a whole woman...."

"I don't know what I am," she said. "I'm something new."

"*Preziosa,*" he said gently, stroking her hair with one hand, his face an indecipherable mixture of sadness, joy and deep longing. "What a precious thing you are." His hand wavered and came to rest at the top fastening of her caftan. He leaned forward and kissed the outer corners of her eyes as he gently unfastened the first few loops.

Rebecca's heart pounded wildly at his touch. "Nick..." she whispered. "Please...don't...." She was suddenly caught between her feelings for him and her fear of this powerful unknown, this inflammatory chemistry between them.

Nick seemed equally confused by her action. "*Cosa significa?*" he asked hoarsely as he caught a lock of her hair between his fingers and kissed the curl at the end. "What is worrying you?"

She shook her head. "I feel so many things at once. I'm all mixed up...I don't know.... Who are you? What am I to you?" She covered her eyes with her hands and laughed softly. "I swore I'd keep this relationship on a professional basis."

"Professional...personal...well...." Nick took her hand and examined it tenderly, tracing the lines, turning over the fingers, as if it were some new thing he'd never seen before. His face was thoughtful. "I'm a director. You're an actress. It's true. We have that relationship." He smiled. "But I'm not just a director. I'm also a man. One doesn't cancel the other. I'm both simultaneously. You and I are artists who happen to be working together; but at the same time, I'm also a man and you're a woman.... We're complex beings and that's the richness of it. Why? Do you feel some conflict? Do you feel that because we know each other professionally we can't know each other personally?''

"I guess maybe I did. Now I don't know.''

"Well, I hope you don't have some nonsensical notion that you're another ingenue being led astray. That would be silly. Whatever happens between us now will not affect the future of the play.''

Rebecca smiled. "It's not that. . . .''

"Then what? What, *cara*? What don't you know?''

"I don't know what you want.''

"I want to carry you off and make glorious love to you.''

"I don't know how you feel. . . .''

Nick gave her an odd look and sighed. He relinquished her hand and scooped up a fistful of sand with his own. "Oh, I see,'' he said. "You want the oaths.''

"The oaths?''

"The oaths. Yes, the oaths. Women always want to hear the oaths.'' He laughed ruefully to himself, pouring the sand back and forth from one hand to the other. "I love you; I'll never love anyone but you; I'll never leave you; forever and ever till death do us part. The oaths.'' He winced and shrugged. "Well, I'm not very big on the oaths. I'm terrific on the here and now, but I'm not very big on the oaths. To me, the oaths are like this. . . .'' He allowed the sand to run through his fingers and back into the earth. "You swear an oath today and mean it with all your heart, but tomorrow you break it. . . or you hold it over your lover's head and you punish them with it. . . or you allow it to petrify and become a dead thing, a stony reminder of something that used to be—a farce.''

Rebecca's heart broke a little when she saw the jaded look that had come into his face. "How'd you get to be so bitter, Nick?'' she asked, as much out of her own pain as anything else, because he'd frightened her and made her feel there could never be any lasting love between them. Then she realized that she knew the answer to her own question and regretted having asked it. Francesca Cini had left her mark all right.

He flashed her a fierce look and then she saw the hood descend. He willfully veiled whatever emotion was burning within him, and in the blink of an eye he was as cool and as graceful and as detached as she had ever seen him. He stood up and offered her his hand. "Come on," he said. "I'll walk you back."

CHAPTER SIX

NICK HAD BEEN RIGHT about one thing. The exchange that had taken place between them on that lonesome beach—an exchange fraught with promise and confusion, with rapturous discovery and sharp disappointment—had absolutely no bearing on the progress of the play. Monday morning they met again at rehearsal, both of them prompt, both of them prepared, both of them polite as two Oriental potentates coming together to fulfill some proscribed ritual. He greeted her. She greeted him. And they settled down to the business at hand. Nick was demanding, encouraging. He gave her no less but no more than the attention she needed. She took his direction and his notes and his suggestions and incorporated them painstakingly into her performance.

She looked at him and her heart rose and fell in her chest like a dolphin, but she merely smiled and said "Yes, sir" and did her job. The word "professional" was acquiring a new dimension in her vocabulary.

It wasn't easy.

It wasn't easy at all.

Alone at home at night, when she was finally able to sit down and listen to what her heart had to say, it went on at length. "Look here," her heart told her, "I think I love that man. I love him so much that I just may keel over and die of it. I love him so much that he can't pick up a pencil or bat an eye or take a breath without my being aware of it. I feel as if he's the middle C on the keyboard and I'm the E and the G, and whenever he comes into a room, we make up a major chord. I love him mightily.

"Which doesn't mean that I like him particularly. I loathe the way he can just shut himself off so that you have no idea what he's thinking or feeling or whether he even remembers who you are from one day to the next. I loathe the way he runs hot and cold. One minute he's inside your mind, thinking your thoughts before you can think them, closer to you than your own breath. The next minute he's on the moon, rocky and airless and inaccessible. Sometimes I just loathe him.

"Which doesn't stop me from continuing to love him, although I wish it did. I love him so much I can't seem to fall into bed with him . . . for the night or a week of nights or even for the rest of rehearsals. Because then there's opening night and then he's on a plane—to New York, to Rome, to wherever he's going. Because he's a twentieth-century nomad who doesn't believe in oaths. Because Francesca Cini met him before I did and burned up his capacity for commitment. Or maybe he never had any to begin with.

"So what are you going to do, girl, about your poor old heart, which is currently stuck between a rock and a hard place?"

"I'm going to go right on doing my job," was Rebecca's answer. "If I can't have his love, I'll have his respect. I'm going to be the best Juliet he's ever seen."

So she went to rehearsal on Tuesday and was impeccable.

And she went to rehearsal on Wednesday and was impeccable.

By Thursday, even this most impeccable of heroines needed some time off.

"NEITHER OF US has to be at the theater until two in the afternoon," she said to Chris Matheson, having roused him from a deep sleep with an early-morning phone call. "Why don't you come over here in about an hour. We'll drive out to the Twin Oaks Ranch and go horseback riding. The place belongs to a fellow named Al Delgado, whom I've known since I was a kid. My brother keeps him supplied with horses and I'm sure he'll let us have a couple for the morning. What do you say?''

He was still half-asleep when he arrived at her door at seven-thirty. His fair hair looked as if it had not seen a comb and his shirt was inside out, but he was game. ''This was a good idea,'' he affirmed as they drove north into the open countryside. ''I needed to do something other than rehearse that bloody play from morning till night. I've got iambic pentameter on the brain.''

''Me, too. I just had to get away from everything and everybody for a few hours.''

''Yeah.'' He yawned. ''Though I must say, for two people who didn't like each other very much, you and Nick are starting to work smoothly together.''

''Aren't we, though.''

''What happened? Did you finally sit down and have a talk and bury the hatchet?''

Rebecca sighed. ''Chris, my friend, I don't want to talk about the show. I don't want to talk about Nick Corelli. I don't want to talk about anything remotely to do with Shakespeare Bay for the next four hours. Okay? This is a holiday.''

''Okay,'' he agreed with a sleepy smile. ''No shop talk.''

Al Delgado was only too happy to lend them horses from his stable at Twin Oaks. The old rancher helped Rebecca saddle a high-spirited mare she had helped to raise from a foal, before introducing Chris to a more docile mount that suited his inexperience. And before very long, they were riding side by side through an open meadow fragrant with the smell of wild flowers and tall grass turning gold beneath the summer sun. Rebecca breathed a sigh of relief. Here in the country, without so much as a highway or a telephone pole in sight, she felt as carefree and unencumbered as the Mendocino tomboy she once had been. She clucked to the mare, gave her a gentle kick and took off at a gallop across the meadow, leaving Chris behind. Her long dark braids snapped out behind her in the wind, and she felt her heart soar with an old excitement. How had she wandered so far from the simplicity of this kind of life? What had possessed her to pursue anything so perversely demanding as an acting career? Or to fall in love with anyone as impossible as Nick Corelli? She didn't know. She didn't care. For a few stolen hours, she was free again.

At last she had to stop for a bit and wait for Chris to catch up. Panting for breath, she leaned forward and patted the animal's neck. "Good girl," she crooned happily as she drank in the sights and sounds around her with the thirst of one who had been away too long. Today the meadow was a study in light and shadow as one high-flying cloud after another flitted across the face of the sun. Bees buzzed amid the late-blooming flowers. The perspiration that had broken out across her upper lip tasted salty and good. In the distance she could see that Chris had finally got into sync with his horse and was making way toward her. "Halloo!" she called, waving one hand above her head.

"Halloo!" he answered, as he joined her once more. He was wide awake now, his cheeks glowing from the exercise, his hair whipped and tousled by the breeze. She was surprised to find herself thinking how handsome he was. Really very handsome. Chris. Once her teenage idol. Now her Romeo. Over the long course of rehearsals, deeply absorbed in her work, mawkishly enamored of Nick the Fiend, she had somehow forgotten just how attractive Chris Matheson was. A Botticelli prince on horseback. Now, why couldn't she fall for someone nice like that?

"Race you to the top of that hill over there!" she yelled, with a saucy flick of her braids. And they were off again. For the next few hours they roamed the generous acreage of Al Delgado's spread. Chris was especially gratified to discover a small sparkling creek hidden in a grove of trees, where he could take off his shoes and wade. Rebecca joined him for a time, and after watering their horses and leaving them to graze, they both stretched out upon the bank and closed their eyes.

Having dozed off in the warm grass for a period of fifteen or twenty minutes, they were rudely awakened by the sting of raindrops pelting across their reclining bodies. Rebecca's eyes flew open in dismay and she scrambled to her feet and stared up at the sky, shielding her face with her hands. The high-flying clouds that had earlier accompanied their trek had now given way to a brooding purplish mass moving in eastward from the ocean. "Just what we need!" she moaned to Chris. "Come on, let's get out of here." They quickly mounted and headed back in the direction of the stables.

They had only gone a few miles when the heavens opened and began to pour in earnest, drenching them both to the skin. The sky was so dark and the rain so blinding that the landscape took on a different look altogether. "Are you sure we came this way?" Chris called to her.

"I can't tell," she shouted back. "I can't see. . . ."

"Look over there." He pointed toward a vaguely squarish shape at the edge of the woods to their left. "Isn't that some kind of shed? I say we get out of this and wait for it to blow over."

"I'm with you," she agreed.

The building proved to be a small abandoned barn, which they had passed earlier during their meanderings. One wall was gone entirely and there was only a dirt floor, but the roof had remained intact and at least offered some shelter from the storm. Feeling grateful indeed for this frail piece of luck, they led the horses inside.

"Please have a seat, your ladyship," Chris said, affecting a hoity-toity British accent. "So kind of you to drop by the country manor. Charming weather we're having, don't you agree?'' Ever the actor, he now seized upon the opportunity to transform their forced encampment into a lighthearted game.

"Charming," she echoed, making a vain attempt to shake herself dry, puppy-dog fashion. "But tell me, milord, where do you suggest I sit?"

"I think you'll find this chaise to your liking," he advised, dusting off a wooden crate, the only such object in the shed. "But do be careful. It's an antique. Priceless, you know. Been in our family for years. Mother's frightfully attached to it."

"Well, if it's so valuable," she minced, playing along with him, "I'm not at all sure I want to sit on it. I'd hate to be responsible for the destruction of an heirloom."

"Oh, it's not the *value* of the thing that concerns me," he countered. "It's the *splinters*. I'd never forgive myself if you got a splinter in . . . that exquisite portion of your pedigreed anatomy."

"Well, since you put it that way . . ." she demurred, perching herself atop the crate as delicately as if she were wearing a tea gown. "But, milord, where will you sit? I mean, I do think it's all very novel and interesting that you only have one piece of furniture in the entire manor, but—"

"There's a reason for that!" he improvised. "The reason being, my dear Lady Peaseblossom, that I shall now be forced by necessity to share the chaise with you." Chris seated himself on the crate next to her and affected a look of smoldering passion.

Rebecca giggled. "Marquis de Marquee! What could you possibly hope to gain by such an action?"

He wiggled his eyebrows. "The better, my little Peaseblossom, to put my arm around your fragile shoulders and protect you from the chill." He did so.

She fluttered her lashes and turned away from him. "You go too far!"

"Too far! I would go to the ends of the earth for a single crumb from your ladyship's tea table! I would walk barefoot to Palestine for the touch of your nether lip!''

"My which lip?" She laughed, barely able to contain her mirth and stay within the confines of the game.

"Your nether lip! Your nether lip!" he rhapsodized, indicating her lower lip with the tip of his finger. "You laugh...but my poor heart is crying out for a single touch of your nether lip!" Sweeping her back into his arms, he kissed her with an hilarious approximation of repressed passion. The crate collapsed and they both fell to the ground. Rebecca lay on her back, giggling helplessly...until she saw the new expression of his face. In an instant, the game had given way to something else entirely. There was a soft serious look about him. The barn was silent, save for the constant drum of rain and the low shuddering whinny of one of the horses. Chris gave her a crooked half smile before he bent and kissed her once more, this time as himself.

When he had done, she looked up at him with a flush of surprise. "What are you doing?" she whispered.

"I don't know," he told her. "Come here and I'll see...." Gathering her into his arms, he sought out her mouth with his own softly parted one. He was sweet, very sweet. She put her arms around his neck and returned the kiss, hoping somehow, by some magic, this action might erase the aching memory of another mouth, another pair of arms. Besides, she really was fond of him. Fond. But—and now she had to admit the truth—not truly attracted to him. Nothing like the way she was to Nick. Chris was, well, he was like Adam to her. Like a brother. She felt herself begin to giggle again and struggled to conceal it for fear of hurting his feelings. How strange to be kissing one's almost-brother in a barn in the rain!

Chris had begun to shake with suppressed laughter, too. At last he could contain himself no longer, and he released her, laughed aloud and sat up. "It really doesn't work, does it?" he asked affectionately.

"No." She shook her head, unable to wipe the silly grin off her face. "It doesn't."

"Becca—I don't want to offend you—but I felt for a moment like I was kissing Mia."

"I felt like I was kissing Adam!"

This sent them both off into an uninterrupted fit of giggles for the next several minutes. At last Chris wiped a tear from his eye and found his voice again. "But I am enormously fond of you, you know. I value your friendship. And I think you're a lovely girl."

"You're lovely, too. I'm glad we're friends."

"Friends, but not...."

"But not...."

"At any rate—" he grinned "—we certainly do act well together."

"Yes," she sighed, holding her aching sides, "there's that."

"Oh! Speaking of which...did I tell you my father is coming up to visit me this week? He's planning to stay till the opening of the show—"

"No!" Rebecca exclaimed with fresh enthusiasm. "That's good news, isn't it?"

"That's very good news. At least to me. It will be the first time we've seen each other in over three years."

"Three years!" Rebecca couldn't imagine going that long without communicating with Adam.

"Well, let's see...." Chris calculated. "I was in London for almost three years, studying, as I told you. Then, when I got back to Los Angeles in January, I called him but he didn't want to see me."

"No?" She was curious but had long since learned not to pry into his private life.

"No. My dad's been through a difficult time in recent years."

"Yes, you told me about your sister's accident...."

"Right. Well, you see, it was dad who took the girls on that river-rafting trip. I was elsewhere and mother didn't want to go, so it was just the three of them. When the boat overturned in the rapids, dad managed to save Mia but not Molly. He could never forgive himself.'' Chris shook his head and gave an ironic little laugh. "For years he'd been playing the part of the perfect father. 'Father Knows Best.' Offscreen, he was a good father, but onscreen he was the *perfect* father. Episode after episode, year after year, he solved every conceivable crisis the writers could devise. Different organizations across the country would send him honorary awards—Father of the Year, that sort of thing, because most of America identified him so heavily with the role he played. After a while, I guess he began to believe it, too. Ben Matheson, Superdad. Then when he couldn't save his own child from drowning, it just destroyed him. He felt like a farce. He gave up acting. There were ongoing problems with Mia, with my mother. He eventually gave up altogether.''

"And now he's coming to visit."

"He's coming to visit under his own steam and it's really far out. You'll have to meet him. I think maybe this is his way of joining the world again." His eyes were shining in a way that allowed her to see how much his father's visit meant to him. She was pleased that he had admitted her into his confidence.

"I'd love to meet him. How do you think he'll like the play? Is Shakespeare his cup of tea?''

"Sure. *Romeo and Juliet* is one he knows by heart. The last thing he did before the accident was a benefit performance of this play. He was Friar Laurence.''

"Well, what do you know?" She smiled. "I'm really happy for you, Chris. I hope everything goes well.''

"Yeah. So do I. I think we all failed one another in some way when Molly died. None of us was strong enough or patient enough or understanding enough of what the others were going through. But maybe it isn't too late for us to forgive one another and be close again, to clean up the past and move on.''

"Hey," she said with a soft smile, "look. Nature agrees with you. It's stopped raining."

BY THE TIME they got the horses back to the stables, it was three-thirty. Rebecca was horrified to realize that they were already an hour and a half late for rehearsal and that it would be at least another half hour before they reached the theater. And what was scheduled for this afternoon? *Act 5 scene 3*, she recalled in panic. Nothing could be worse. It was a crowd scene. Almost everyone in the company would have been summoned at two and would be there waiting for them to show up, unable to rehearse properly without them. Nick would be livid. He would be beside himself. He would tolerate no excuses. She dared not even envision the trouble to come. Promptness was not merely a courtesy in the theater; it was a covenant. "What are we going to do?" she asked Chris with a quaver in her voice.

"You help Al with the horses," he told her. "I'll go inside and call the theater and tell them what's happened."

But when he returned, he was frowning. "No luck," he said. "I tried three times, but the lines were busy. I think we'd better drive straight there and make our apologies." Al graciously waved them on their way, commiserating about the bad weather and offering to finish up in the stable by himself. Rebecca and Chris thanked him and piled into the Volkswagen. She would have been tempted to speed, but the confounded thing wouldn't exceed fifty miles an hour.

When she saw the expression on Nick's face as they straggled into the rehearsal hall at five past four, she wished she had never come back at all. If looks could kill, she thought. If looks could turn to stone. The room was painfully quiet. All eyes were upon them. The twenty-odd actors who had been attempting to rehearse the final scene of the play stood motionless, frozen in mid-gesture, waiting to see what might give.

It was Harry Moss, the stage manager, who broke the silence. Dressed in a rehearsal skirt, lying corpselike upon the funeral bier, he had obviously been standing in for Rebecca. "Well, thank God," he said, sitting up and unbuttoning his shirt. "I was beginning to feel like a complete sissy."

"I have to apologize," Chris said, stepping forth into the center of the room, "to everyone here, but most of all to you, Nick. I know there's no real excuse for missing a rehearsal and hanging everyone up like this, but I'll tell you what happened anyway." In a few brief sentences he recounted their misadventure and his attempts to phone in. "I'm aware that you can't work too easily without me at this point," he acknowledged. "You have my word that it won't happen again."

"I can only repeat what Chris has said," Rebecca chimed in, feeling about six inches tall. "I'm really very sorry."

"Well," Nick said at last, his voice cool, even, scary. "You're right about one thing. There *are* no real excuses for missing a call. Whose idea was it, anyway, to leave town and go horseback riding before an important rehearsal?"

"Mine," Rebecca admitted.

"It sounds like the sort of outing where any number of accidents might have occurred to prevent your getting here, wouldn't you say?"

"Possibly, but . . . I didn't anticipate . . . ."

"I see." He studied his clipboard for a moment. No one was breathing. She could tell that he was making an effort to control his temper. *Oh, just take out a gun and shoot me,* she thought. *Get it over with, for heaven's sake.* But he wasn't through. Not yet, anyway. "This is Thursday, June 9, is it not?" he asked in the same quiet stony voice.

Everyone nodded.

"And when do we open this show?"

"The fifteenth, Wednesday," Rebecca told him, although she knew the question was rhetorical.

"Less than a week," he concluded. "*Less than a week*. The tickets are sold. The people are coming. We have an obligation to fulfill. As you all know, tomorrow we start rehearsing on the set at the amphitheater. There are going to be a whole host of adjustments, transferring the show from the rehearsal hall up to the mountain. By tomorrow, you're going to be so busy getting used to the costumes and the set and the lights and the music that there isn't going to be a chance to work out the nuances of this scene. This is our last opportunity. If we don't nail it down now, it won't get done. So I'm going to have to ask everyone to remain an extra two hours, if possible. If any of you have a problem, try to work it out with Harry."

Everyone moaned and groaned, but in the end they agreed to stay. Rebecca felt guiltier than ever. And to make matters worse, she was most uncomfortable with her damp hair and her damp clothes, which she had not dared take the time to go home and change. And now, of course, it was too late. She was in no position to complain. She accepted the rehearsal skirt from Harry and took her place upon the bier for the top of the action.

The first half of the scene presented no difficulties. She merely had to lie there and pretend to be dead while one person after another burst into the "tomb" and wept over her limp body. She closed her eyes and folded her hands over her chest, glad to shut out the sight of Nick Corelli sitting across the room with furrowed brow and fiery eye. *Oh!* she thought to herself angrily. *In one day I've managed to erase all the good of the past week! Here I was priding myself on how professional I'd become, on what a dedicated reliable actress I was. In one day my name is mud and I'm an amateur all over again. And that bear, that perfectionistic bastard, that hopelessly beloved man will never let me forget it.*

When it came time for Juliet to wake from her deathlike sleep and discover Romeo's body poisoned at her feet, Rebecca did not have to fake the tears. They came rolling down her cheeks as she choked her way through the lines, weeping not so much for Juliet's plight as for her own. The audience never knew the difference. "That was terrific," one of the other actors whispered to her when the scene was done. "I wish I could cry on cue."

"Let's take it again from the top," was all Nick had to say.

Rebecca pressed her forehead into the palm of her hand and sighed. Suddenly she was very, very tired. Tired and sick at heart. She resumed her place upon the bier and waited for the scene to begin, feeling as if she were trapped within a nightmare in which she was doomed to repeat the same action over and over again. She gathered her skirts around her and shivered. The lingering chill of the rain had crept inward to her bones.

Once again Chris entered the tomb, wept over her body and then poisoned himself. Once again she awoke and discovered him unconscious at her feet. Once again the tears came easily. But this time she couldn't remember the lines.

"Poison, I see, hath been his timeless end," prompted Harry Moss, after a substantial pause.

"Poison, I see, hath been his timeless end," echoed Rebecca. But what came next? She didn't know. Her mind was a complete blank.

"O churl! Drunk all and left no friendly drop to help me after?" Harry offered.

She sneezed.

"What's the matter, Rebecca?" It was Nick speaking now, his voice sounding very thick and far away, like a voice in a dream.

"Nothing," she told him. "I'm fine. I just went up on the lines."

"All right," he grumbled. "Back up a little bit and start again."

The room was so warm. *Someone really ought to*

open a door, she thought. *Too many people in one room breathing up all the air.* She lay down upon the bier and tried to concentrate. Someone gave her a cue. She rose and went through the motions of discovering Romeo's body as they had rehearsed. But try though she might, she could not recall a single line of her speech.

"Okay," she heard Nick say. "Take five, everyone." In an instant he was by her side, pressing his palm against her forehead and her flushed cheeks. "Just what I thought," he observed bitterly. "You've got a fever. You're burning up."

"No." She shook her head in alarm. "I'm okay. I'm just...absentminded. I'll be all right in a minute."

"Harry," Nick ordered. "Haven't you got a thermometer around here somewhere?"

"Sure thing." Harry Moss vanished for an instant and then reappeared, shaking a thermometer, which he placed under Rebecca's tongue. She wondered ruefully how he managed to be so efficient. Did he carry a first-aid kit in that omnipresent briefcase of his?

"A hundred and two," Nick pronounced. "I could wring your neck, Rebecca."

"I feel fine," she insisted stubbornly. "I can still rehearse."

"No, you can't," he retorted. "I'm sending you home. Pronto."

"I won't go. I need this rehearsal. We all need this rehearsal. I can do it."

"Don't argue with me." He gave her a dark look. "At this point, you'll do what I bloody well tell you to do."

"But—"

"Haven't I tried to impress upon you time and time again how important it is to take care of yourself? This isn't just any profession. This is a profession that demands physical strength, stamina, lots of it. You can't just be in fair shape, you have to be in top shape!

Playing a lead in a Shakespearean play is like com-
peting in the Olympics. It is just as much your responsibility to stay in good health as it is to learn your
lines." He raked his hands through his hair in exasperation. She could see that barely suppressed
temper of his start to skyrocket. "Talent isn't
enough!" he raged on. "It isn't enough. You have to
have the discipline! You have to take responsibility for
a lot of things you never thought of before! Don't you
see that you're jeopardizing not only your own work
but my work, and the work of everyone involved in
this show? We're opening in six days and you're so
feverish you can't even rehearse—thanks to your own
folly. I have no sympathy for you. None."

"I didn't plan to get caught in a rainstorm," she
snapped defensively.

"You didn't *plan*." His jaw was taut with anger.
"Did you stop to think whether that might be too risky
an outing just before a big rehearsal? And after you
were drenched, did you take care to see that you didn't
catch cold? Did you dry yourself? Get some warm
clothes? Did you?"

"I was late," she protested. "I didn't have the
time."

"The time...." He shook his head. "This afternoon you lost two hours. But now, thanks to your
negligence, you're going to lose a whole day. You
can't come to rehearsal tomorrow. Look at you—
you're a mess. Now, I want you to go home and go to
bed. I don't want to see you for the next twenty-four
hours." He dismissed her with a disdainful gesture.
"At this moment, I don't want to see you at all. Now
go on. Get out of here. I have work to do."

WHAT FOLLOWED WAS a lonely night filled with tears
and self-reproach, with tirades against Nick and
against herself. How could she have been so stupid?
So luckless? How could he be so unfeeling? She de-
served his scorn. She didn't deserve his scorn. She'd

never open in the show. She would open in the show and be so unthinkably good that he'd be stunned and regret his harsh words. She loved him. She couldn't stand him. On and on.

Only Samcat was there to listen. The hugely pregnant animal lay on the foot of the bed and regarded her with a wise and languorous eye as if to say, "Humans! What do they know?"

At last the fever overtook her and she slept.

In the morning, her temperature was just below a hundred and one and she felt encouraged. She called the theater and asked to speak to Nick. Advised that he was in a meeting, she told the secretary that she was much better and to please ask if she could come to the afternoon rehearsal at the amphitheater. The woman promised to relay her request and call her back with Nick's response. Rebecca padded into the kitchen and downed a large glass of orange juice, confident that all would be made right.

But the order came back, the secretary quoting Nick word for word: "Absolutely not. Stay where you are. We don't need you. We have everything under control."

She climbed mournfully back into bed and pulled the covers over her head. "We don't need you." How desolate those words made her feel. Everyone would be convening on the mountain, full of excitement and high spirits, glad to be on the actual set at last. She could see the picture now and longed desperately to be part of it. The actors would be scampering over the amphitheater, taking turns testing the acoustics, sitting convivially together beneath the blue sky, sharing thermoses of honeyed camomile tea—so good for the throat—and telling one another stories about openings of other shows. And then Nick would begin rehearsal. They would all attack the play with renewed energy, renewed enthusiasm, feeling the sap within them rise in anticipation of opening night.

"We don't need you."

Everyone is replaceable.

She fell into a dark dream, her limbs swollen thick and terribly heavy with the weight of unseen things.

She was sitting in the audience at the amphitheater on opening night, waiting for the show to begin. The lights went down and rose again, illuminating the stage in a golden glow. A hush fell over the audience. Evany Pace, resplendent in the rose-colored Juliet gown, entered to thunderous applause. Rebecca was aghast but could not find her voice in time to protest, to tell the others that some mistake had been made, that it was she, Rebecca, who should be there instead. Then Nick swept onto the stage, dressed as Romeo, carrying a bouquet of roses, and knelt at Evany's feet. "Ahh," she heard someone next to her murmur. "She's the leading lady of his heart."

Rebecca woke with a start and sat up in bed, holding her head in her hands. For a moment she had to struggle to get her bearings. She looked blankly around the sunny disheveled room in which she lay. Curtains fluttered in the breeze. Samcat dozed upon the windowsill. The bedspread had fallen in a heap on the floor. Her riding clothes were strewn across a chair where she had left them the night before. She breathed a sigh of relief. She was safe on Perry's houseboat. It was okay. It had only been a dream.

And what a silly dream, she told herself. There was no truth in it at all. Evany had not taken over her role. Nick was not playing Romeo. And he was not in love with Evany Pace, as he had made clear over dinner at the beach house. It had only been the product of her foolish feverish mind, something she had conjured up to scare herself with. She climbed out of bed and stumbled groggily onto the back deck for some fresh air. If only he would let her go to rehearsal. If only she weren't cooped up in this house, alone with her own doubts and fears.

By evening she could stand it no longer. Her temperature was down to a hundred. She took a shower and dressed with the intention of driving up to the amphitheater. She would arrive just as everyone was coming back from their dinner break for the second runthrough. She would find Nick and talk him into letting her go on. He needed her. He had to. Her understudy—flighty, flaky, young Holly McVee—would be making a mess of things. Nick would be only too glad to have her back. She pulled on a light jacket with a hood—so that he couldn't fault her for dressing inadequately—and headed for the door.

When she reached the parking lot on the mountain, she could tell by the distant strains of music that the rehearsal was already under way. *They must have started early,* she deduced. *That's the music for the ball.* She locked the car and hurried along the footpath that led to the upper rim of the amphitheater.

The play was winding toward the close of the first act. Rebecca stepped out of the shelter of the trees and caught her breath in delight at the sight before her. The set had been finished and shone like a Renaissance vision beneath the magic of the stage lights. The actors were dressed half in their own clothes and half in costumes—a cape here, a pair of high-topped boots there, a plumed hat to give a sense of what it would all look like in the end. Just now they were finishing the dance in which Romeo and Juliet meet and talk for the first time. Rebecca craned her neck to see if Holly McVee had been allowed to wear the rose-colored gown.

At last she spotted her. Only it wasn't Holly McVee leaning upon Chris's arm and delivering the lines Rebecca knew so well. It was Evany Pace.

She was suddenly weak in the knees and had to sit down on one of the stone seats near the back of the theater. Where was Holly McVee? If Rebecca was ill, then Holly should, by all rights, be rehearsing in her place. Where was she? What was going on? Was this yet another dream and would she once again wake to find herself lying in bed in the houseboat?

She pinched the flesh on her arm. It hurt. This was no dream. Evany Pace had, in fact, gone on as Juliet that evening. And what's more, she apparently knew the lines. Rebecca could see that she was not carrying a script.

With a trembling hand Rebecca drew the hood up over her head and sat quietly in the back row, watching the other actress's performance. The woman was not half-bad, she decided as a cold sweat broke out across her upper lip and forehead. From this distance Evany appeared much younger than she actually was. It was possible to believe that she was a young girl at her first ball. She was not implausible in the role. And she was certainly giving it her all.

Rebecca looked around for Nick. There he was in the first row, sitting between Harry Moss and Maggie. "If I decide to fire you, you'll be the first to know. I'm a very direct person," he had once told her. Surely, surely, he had not surreptitiously replaced her!

Yet, he had sent a message only that morning saying, "We don't need you. We have everything under control." What was she to think? At that moment the act came to a close and Nick sprang enthusiastically to his feet. He leaped onto the stage and gathered Chris and Evany to him, throwing an arm over each one's shoulder and speaking excitedly. Chris laughed and nodded his head, and after a moment, excused himself from this little powwow. Nick stood there smiling, holding Evany by both hands, before he leaned over and kissed her on the cheek.

Rebecca heard someone behind her giggle. Two girls from the costume department had come by to watch the rehearsal. "Isn't she beautiful?" one of them gossiped to her friend. "I hear he's crazy about her."

CHAPTER SEVEN

"I COULD ALWAYS GO BACK to Mendocino," she told Samcat as they sat together on the deck of the houseboat, watching the morning light play upon the water. "I could go into business with Adam. I'm sure he could use the help. Maybe I'd build a little cabin of my own. I could spend the rest of my life living in the wilderness, raising horses; it wouldn't be so bad. The country's beautiful up there, you know. I'd never marry. I'd become very solitary and eccentric. I'd always have my freedom and I'd never have to answer to anybody or be jealous of anybody or worry one way or the other what anybody thought of me. I could be happy by myself."

Samcat yawned.

Rebecca smiled at the animal's rude assessment of her proposition and took a sip of her coffee. She had risen with the sun that morning. Unable to bear the sight of Evany and Nick, unable to cope with the avalanche of her own emotions, she had returned home, feeling as if she had just witnessed the death of all her hopes. She had slept erratically and eaten little. The only good news was that her fever had passed and her temperature was back to normal. She was physically fit, if not happy.

"Okay—" she nudged Samcat with the edge of her foot "—what about this? I don't go back to Mendocino and become a rancher like my brother. No! I go to New York and pay my dues and work odd jobs and then, before too long, I get my big break as an actress. I become the toast of Broadway. Playboys and princes line up outside my dressing-room door. One day Nick Corelli sees my face on the cover of a magazine and realizes that I'm the only woman who could ever star in his plays or in his life. He calls and begs me to see him. But it's too late. I'm tied up for the next sixty years.''

The cat gave her a bored look and closed its eyes.

"No good, huh?" Rebecca said, feeling her heart sink once more under the weight of her own depression. "Then what? What do you think I should do?"

She heard the telephone ring inside the house. "Answer the phone," she said aloud. "I should answer the phone." She wound her way into the bedroom and caught the telephone on the fifth ring.

"So where are you?" Nick's husky voice growled on the other end. "I said you had twenty-four hours to get well. That's it. Time's up. How's your fever?"

"Gone."

"Well, I should hope so. Listen, I need you here an hour early this morning. Some people are coming over from one of the San Francisco papers to take pictures of you and Chris, and I want you to be finished by ten so we can start rehearsal on time, okay? We've got a lot of work to do today and I don't want us to fall behind. Now I hope you're not kidding me about the fever. You are well, aren't you?"

"Strong as a horse," she answered quaveringly, amazed at what she was hearing.

"Horse. . ." he muttered. "If I so much as catch you around a horse, heads are going to roll. No horseback riding, no rainstorms, no *niente* for you until this play is over. Now get dressed and get down here."

WHEN SHE LOOKED BACK at the end of a long blissfully tiring day of rehearsals, she felt as if she had been granted a reprieve. Her twenty-four-hour exile from Shakespeare Bay had seemed to last a lifetime. It had served to show her just how much her new profession meant to her. She had the theater in her blood all right.

She could no more give it up and become a lonely hermit than she could give up breathing or eating.

The rehearsals on the mountain were sheer delight. Working out in the open air on the new set seemed to inspire the whole company. By the evening's run-through, they were performing in full costume. The cues for lighting and music had been carefully synchronized and helped to feed the actors' belief in their own performances. The play had suddenly come alive in a fresh exhilarating way. Rebecca gave herself to her role with new abandon.

It was as if all her bad dreams had dwindled and diminished with the passing of her fever. Well, almost all of them. Nick was still distant; when he was not giving her direction, he had very little to say to her. On the supper break he had gone off with Evany and Gabe, declining an invitation to dine with the rest of the company. Later, the three of them had reappeared arm in arm, laughing over some joke, their heads close together.

When she had a chance to talk to Chris alone, she told him about her secret visit to the amphitheater the night before and about her day and night spent in purgatory over the thought that she had been dismissed. "Was I crazy to feel that way?" she asked him. "Why was Evany rehearsing in my place?"

"Well. . ." he said musingly. "I don't think you're crazy. If you're crazy, then all actors are crazy, because everyone worries about being replaced. And it does occasionally happen, even to the best of actors. Katharine Hepburn was fired time and time again when she was first starting out. I guess you just have to stay cool and do your best and try not to let your fears run away with you. About Evany—" he chuckled "—well, I guess you haven't heard the news."

"What?" she demanded.

"On the same day we were caught in that rainstorm, Holly McVee ran off with one of the other actors—you know, whatsisname, the fellow who plays the apothecary and understudies Friar Laurence. Nobody knows where they've gone or whether they've eloped or what. It's the latest scandal. Anyway, when you and I didn't show up for rehearsal and Nick discovered that Holly and the apothecary had vanished as well, he really hit the ceiling. He felt like the whole show was falling to pieces around him. No wonder he was so ticked off when we finally straggled in.''

"Oh no!" Rebecca gasped. "So he had no one to cover me...."

Chris wiggled his eyebrows. "Which brings us back to Ms Pace. She immediately went to Nick and told him that she knew the role. And she does. She'd learned it, every single line. It's pretty spooky. Listen, sugar, I'm glad you're well and I think you'd better stay well, because that lady is primed and ready to step into your shoes. She's done her homework. Of course, Nick was glad to use her for the runthrough yesterday. She really got him out of a pinch.''

"Wow," Rebecca breathed, feeling a little chill run up the back of her neck. "She's really calculating, isn't she?"

Chris laughed. "That's a polite way of putting it. And not only is she calculating, but she's beautiful and reasonably talented and she's absolutely obsessed with Nicky. Haven't you noticed the way she sticks to him like glue?''

Rebecca shrugged. "He seems to encourage her. I don't see him telling her to take a walk, do you?''

"No," Chris agreed. "But what do you care if she goes out with him? You've still got the part, don't you? That's all that really matters.''

"Yes," Rebecca echoed hollowly. "That's all that really matters.''

"THIS IS HOPELESS," she muttered to herself when she woke up dreaming of Nick Corelli on Sunday morning, her arms wrapped around her pillow. "This is no good. I don't know how I'm going to do it, but I've got to get him out of my system. The only question is, how do you fall out of love once you've fallen in?" She rolled over sleepily and looked at the clock. Ten-thirty. "Well, small wonder. This was the first full night of sleep she'd had in several days.

Samcat padded heavily into the room, crying for attention. Rebecca stumbled out of bed and made her way into the kitchen, yawning and rubbing her eyes. The cat followed noisily upon her heels, evidently in some distress.

"Okay, okay," Rebecca mumbled. "One bowl of cat chow coming up."

But when she had opened a can and knelt to spoon the contents into the animal's dish, she found that Samcat still had plenty of food left over from the night before. "What's the matter with you, Bozo?" she inquired. "Was the entrée not to your liking? Do you want something else? Is that it?" With a sigh she emptied the dish into the trash and refilled it with fresh food.

Samcat ignored the proffered meal but continued to cry and pace back and forth in front of her. "What is it?" Rebecca asked impatiently. "Speak English." Then the realization dawned on her. "Oh, my gosh, are you ready to have those kittens? Is that what you're up to?" She reached out and scratched the animal's head, wondering if there was anything she ought to do.

She went to the phone and dialed Chris Matheson. He had always taken a great interest in Samcat and her impending motherhood. He answered at once, his voice clear and cheery as if he had been up for hours. "I think Samcat's about to deliver," she said. "What should I do?"

"Nothing much you can do," he answered. "Did you fix a box for her?"

"No. Was I supposed to? Listen, I'm a horse person, not a cat person."

"If you don't want her to give birth in one of your

dresser drawers, I'd suggest you put some old rags into a box for her. I'm coming over."

"Good," she said. "Hurry."

She followed his advice and created a makeshift nest for Samcat in a cardboard box, into which the animal gratefully climbed at once. Rebecca had scarcely enough time to shower and slip into a pair of jeans and a red plaid shirt before Chris was knocking at her door. "Did I miss anything?" he inquired anxiously.

"No." She laughed. "The mother-to-be is in the box in the corner. Would you like coffee? I've got English muffins."

"Wonderful," he said, smiling. "I'm glad you called."

Less than two hours later, Samcat lay surrounded by five new kittens, ugly and blind as little mice. "They'll look better in a few days—once they open their eyes," Chris reassured Rebecca. "In a couple of weeks or so, they'll be cute. They'll climb out of that box and run all over the houseboat. What are you going to call them?"

"I don't know," she said. "Kitty, kitty, kitty, kitty and kitty."

"No," he protested. "You have to give them all names." He put his arm around her shoulders and began to lecture her playfully. "You're their godmother. You'll have to christen them. We'll have a christening party and invite everyone from Shakespeare Bay. Maybe that way we'll find homes for them all."

Rebecca giggled and rested her head on his shoulder. "Okay. But I'll leave the arrangements to you. You're their uncle."

"Excuse me," said a third voice. Rebecca recognized it at once and her heartbeat quickened. As she turned slowly around to face the open doorway, she saw Nick Corelli standing there, silhouetted by the morning sunshine. There was a scowl on his face.

"Nick." Her voice wavered even as she spoke his name. "Come in."

"I was in the neighborhood," he announced brusquely. "I thought I'd drop by and see how you were. Hello, Chris."

"Signore Director," Chris greeted him jovially. Did he too sense the sudden tension in the air, Rebecca wondered.

"Come and see what Samcat has brought forth this morning," Chris continued.

Nick stepped inside and moved around to join them at the foot of the cardboard box. "Kittens..." he muttered. Apparently, the sight of the squirming squeaking brood failed to soften his heart in the smallest degree. He was clearly in a temper about something, though Rebecca could not guess exactly what.

Chris shifted uneasily from one foot to the other. "Well," he said, "time for me to be off."

"Must you go?" Rebecca put in hurriedly. "How about another cup of coffee?"

"Don't go on my account," Nick told him emphatically. "I'm not staying."

Chris surveyed Nick and Rebecca with an odd look that said he thought they'd both gone a little mad. "I have to pick up my father at the airport at two," he said lightly as he moved toward the door. "Bye Samcat, Becca. See you tomorrow, Nick."

When he was gone, Rebecca stood for a moment, gazing blindly at the door, uncertain of what to do next. Nick sat on the arm of the sofa and studied his hands. No one spoke. "Well," she said at last, "can I offer you some coffee?"

"No thanks," he said coolly. "I just came by to see how you were. How are you?"

"Fine."

"Fever gone?"

"Yes, thanks."

"You're sure?"

"Yes, I'm sure!" she said testily, buckling under the strain of their monosyllabic conversation. "For goodness' sake, Nick, you make me feel like a prize pony. Would you like to see my teeth? Check out my hooves?''

"Look," he said with an unmistakable note of sarcasm in his voice, "calm down, will you? I didn't mean to run your boyfriend off."

"Chris isn't my boyfriend," Rebecca told him flatly. "He's my friend."

"Oh, come on, Becca. You don't have to pretend anymore. It's been common knowledge ever since the two of you failed to show up for rehearsal."

Her mouth fell open. She couldn't believe what she was hearing.

"I guess it's only natural, you and Matheson," Nick continued maddeningly. "You're the natural choice for each other. You're both about the same age. Both of you so young. Full of big romantic ideas about life. It's only natural that you would eventually get carried away with the roles you play and move in together."

"You don't know what you're talking about!" Rebecca felt her own temper suddenly break free. "And besides, what right have you to come in here and start making insinuations? It's none of your business."

"It becomes my business when you go off on a romantic adventure and get into the kind of trouble you did the other day!"

"What's the matter with you?" she demanded. "We've both apologized and done our best to make amends. For your information, Chris Matheson is not my roommate or my boyfriend or anything else. Now you can accept that or not—it's entirely up to you. Good heavens, if I didn't know better, I'd think you were jealous."

"I'm not jealous!" he fired back. "But you can't expect me to believe—"

"I don't care what you believe," she announced hotly. "You're such a total cynic, you wouldn't know the truth if it walked up and sat on you."

"I'm not a cynic," he countered. "I'm a realist."

"Oh, how can I even talk to you?" she cried, no longer able to control what she was saying. "You baffle me, do you know that? One day I feel close to you. The next day it's as if we've never met. And the next, you come in here, asking personal questions and making all kinds of judgments and assessments as if you had some kind of stake in my life. Well, I've answered your questions, only you're so damn mistrustful that you can't conceive that someone just might be telling you the truth. Why don't you go home, Nick? I don't think we really have anything to talk about. I'm over my flu and I'm back on the job and I'm doing my absolute best in the role. That's all you really care about, isn't it? Please, go home."

Nick's face was a mask of ice as he turned on his heel and strode out the front door, slamming it behind him. Rebecca sank into the nearest chair, astonished by her audacity. She brought one hand shakily up to her forehead and closed her eyes. She wondered if she would ever see Nick Corelli again outside the proscribed ritual of rehearsal.

In twenty minutes he was back. "All right," he told her, coming on board before she could protest. "Maybe I was."

"Was what?" she asked uncomprehendingly.

"What you said." He shrugged. He avoided looking her in the eye. "Jealous."

An odd little smile played at the corners of her mouth. "Am I hearing you right?" she asked. "Would you say that again?"

"Maybe I was jealous. Maybe I was," Nick repeated. He paced restlessly back and forth in front of her as if he were struggling with this new revelation. Obviously her words had had an impact. "I've...." He paused for a moment as if unwilling to go on. Rebecca sat there in wonderment. At last he continued. "I've had you on my mind. I woke up this morning and realized that I had been dreaming about you. Something prompted me to get in my car and come over here and so I did. And the first thing I saw was Matheson with his arm around you. I guess you could say I was jealous. It's crazy, I know."

Rebecca shook her head and laughed softly. Nick's second visit was proving even more surprising than his first.

"I don't like this." Nick made a face as if he'd just experienced a bad taste in his mouth. "I'm not a jealous person. At least, I haven't been, not in a long time. Oh, no..." he sighed.

"Why 'oh no'?" she asked.

"Are you some kind of witch, Becca? Have you put some kind of spell on me with those lovely witch eyes?"

"No," she demurred. "I'm no witch."

"Sure you are," Nick insisted. "Why else would I go out and buy a bottle of champagne and a whole basket of picnic food like I just did?"

"You bought what?"

"A picnic," he said. "I hope you don't have plans. The champagne's getting warm out in the car at this very minute. We should leave. That is, if you're not still mad."

"I don't know," she said, quite overwhelmed by his sudden change in attitude. "I guess I'm not."

"Good." He grinned. "Because you shouldn't be. Remember when I got back from New York? You did the same thing. You accused me of committing every sin known to man with Evany Pace. Remember? You thought the absolute worst of me."

"You're right," Rebecca conceded, her heart beginning to flutter like a bird. "I was almost as bad as you."

"Worse," Nick said. His eyes had begun to glow with a soft warm light. "Were you jealous?"

"Terribly," she confessed.

"Will you come on a picnic to Angel Island with me now?"

"I thought you said I wasn't allowed any more outings until the show opens," she teased.

"I called the weather station," he said, and grinned. "Sunny skies all day."

They drove to the neighboring town of Tiburon and caught the ferry over to the island—a lovely wooded state park in the middle of San Francisco Bay. During the ten-minute ride, they passed scores of sailboats and small yachts; everyone, it seemed, had come out to take advantage of the glorious sky-blue day. Gulls followed in the wake of the boat, occasionally diving for a crust of bread tossed overboard by one of the passengers. Rebecca leaned against the railing in mute happiness, as Nick stood beside her, shielding her against the wind with his body.

Soon they were docking in Ayala Cove. Nick picked up the basket and followed her down the gangplank to the pier. At his insistence they bypassed the populated area, where other visitors were sunning themselves on the beach or lounging in the grass, and found their own private secluded spot atop a tree-covered hill overlooking the water. Nick spread out the old blanket they had brought with them from the houseboat and opened the bottle of champagne.

"Let's have some now," he suggested. "Quick while it's still cold." He poured two glasses and offered her one.

"What shall we drink to?" she asked gaily.

"To you," he said. "To your terrible temper and your bewitching eyes and your great success in the play."

She laughed and sipped the wine. It was dry, subtle, fizzy, the perfect complement to this sparkling afternoon. The sun shone down diamondlike upon the bay. In the distance they could see the bright white houses dotting the hillsides of Sausalito and Tiburon. White houses, white sails, white gulls, white clouds. A champagne Sunday. She felt her own high spirits bubble up and spill over. "Now it's my turn," she announced, lifting her glass for another toast. "To you, Nick Corelli, whoever you may be."

"Don't you know?" he asked, a wry smile framing what seemed to be a real question. "Don't you know yet who I am?"

"No," she told him with a merry shrug. "You're a mystery to me. You change from moment to moment. From day to day. I never know what to expect. The only thing I can count on is your unpredictability. It's the one constant thing about you." She saluted him and took another sip of the champagne.

"Really?" He lounged on the blanket, propping himself up on one elbow, and squinted back at her. He seemed genuinely perplexed. "Am I so hidden?"

She nodded vigorously. "Hidden. Hidden."

"Damn." He frowned, then shook his head. "Well, you may be right. I suppose it's a habit I've fallen into. I don't mean to shut you out, Rebecca."

"Don't," she echoed. "Don't shut me out."

"I didn't shut you out this morning," he mused, "did I? If I remember correctly, I made a complete fool of myself!" He laughed, then winced at the memory. "I told you how jealous I was. I confessed! There! Weren't you satisfied? Isn't that what you wanted?"

"Yes." She grinned and went on, "But I want more. I want to know you, Nick Corelli. I want to know who you are."

He studied her face for a long moment, his eyes dark and burning. She sensed that he was struggling to put something into words and waited quietly, eagerly, to see what it might be. Nick extended his hand toward her face and then withdrew it. It was an awkward gesture. It was the only awkward thing she had ever seen him do. She was oddly moved.

I love you, she thought. *What is in your head? Tell me.*

But, at last, out of some inner frustration with himself, he gave up the attempt. He laughed and said in a voice that was half-joking and half-serious, "You asked me who I am? Well, I'm a starving man, *cara*. On a number of levels. Let's start with the simplest." Sitting up, he reached for the picnic basket.

Rebecca wondered at the moment that had just passed between them, so full of unsaid things. She knew there were levels to this man that she had never even glimpsed. She watched him now as he delved into the basket and brought out one miraculous dish after another. There was caviar and an elegant array of cheeses; deviled eggs, a marinated salad and wafer-thin slices of rare roast beef. And, for dessert, strawberries. Nick, ever the magician, ever the conjurer, produced each one with a flourish.

"Ta-da!" he announced. "Where would you like to begin?"

Rebecca reached for the cheese knife.

"Oh, no, you don't!" he chided her. "You stay where you are." He graciously served her cream cheese and caviar, making a game of feeding her the first bite out of his own hand. What she could not finish herself, he devoured readily. Dish by dish, glass by glass, the afternoon stretched happily on. It was the slowest, most luxurious feast she could have imagined.

"Open wide," he told her, wafting a strawberry before her face. "Here it comes, ready or not."

She gulped down the last morsel of food still in her mouth and opened her lips just in time to receive the berry. He had made her laugh so hard that she almost choked on it. She wiped a tear from the corner of her eye and patted her chest with her hand.

"Don't laugh," he scolded her playfully. "This is serious business! Savor! Savor!"

The berry was sweet and ripe, perfectly in season. She rolled her eyes upward in ecstasy.

"Delizioso, no?" he asked.

"Delicious, *sì*!" she told him as soon as she could speak. "Here, you try one!" Following his lead, she

picked up another strawberry and maneuvered it zig-
zag fashion into his mouth. He accepted it, catching
her by the wrist and nibbling the tips of her fingers as if
to relish every last taste.

The sensuous action of his mouth caused Rebecca
to blush. At first, this was manifested only as a hot
tingling in her cheeks and she hoped that he would not
notice. But when he caught her eye, she could feel the
color begin to spread up to the roots of her hair and
down into her neck. His eyes crinkled into a smile, and
wickedly, mischievously, he held tight to her hand and
took the thumb into his mouth, grazing it with his
teeth as if it were a particularly attractive morsel he
was considering devouring. Rebecca was crimson. At
last she had to look away.

"Wonderful," Nick murmured. "You blush better
than anyone I know." He reached over and lifted her
head gently by the chin, forcing her to look at him
once more. Slowly, reluctantly, she raised her eyes,
fearing that he would now see just how much she loved
him, how much she wanted him. For a long moment
they remained suspended, locked in each other's gaze.
Nick's face underwent a subtle transformation as if he
had read her innermost thoughts. She saw the hard
line next to his mouth soften and fade away. His eyes
grew bright with feeling. He suddenly looked very
young, as if some of the old mistrust had somehow left
him. At last, he leaned forward and kissed her. He
tasted of strawberry. But that was not all. There was a
new sweetness there that surprised and touched her.
She put her arms around his neck and held him close.

For a moment all she knew was the inner sound of
their hearts beating together, an intimate, insistent
music.

Then Nick gently lowered her onto her back. She
felt her head come to rest against the blanket as his
arms encircled her. The weight of him was dark and
sweet against her. She opened her mouth to say his
name but he was already there.

He took possession of her mouth in a way that almost frightened her. She was aware of some great need in him that she had never experienced before. There was a deep, all-encompassing hunger that pulled at her, body and soul. It was almost as if he might consume her, as if she might disappear into him forever. She felt the edges of her being soften and dissolve. Time bled into eternity.

Nick rolled to one side and suddenly she was on top of him, her long dark hair cascading around them like a veil. "Look at you," he said. "So beautiful." He placed a hand on each of her temples and laced his fingers into her hair. She turned her face to one side and kissed the palm of his hand.

"Becca...."

"Yes?" she whispered.

"You are...so tender...." The look on his face was strangely vulnerable. "You kiss me as if you care."

"As if?" She smiled. "How else would I kiss you?"

He breathed a long deep sigh and gathered her against his chest. "*Preziosa*, I think it's your tenderness that frightens me the most."

"Frightens you?" She was astonished. "What do you mean?"

His hands caressed the length of her body, a reverence and an intensity in his touch. It was as if he were a sculptor, intent on molding their intertwined forms into one. "When it comes to love," he said, "some people demand...some seduce...some manipulate.... But you are so very tender. Sometimes the softest things have the greatest power. I am steeled against everything but the power of your tenderness."

She searched his face in wonderment. "What are you saying?"

"What am I saying?" His arms tightened around her for a moment and she felt a surge of emotion pass through him. Then he abruptly released her and sat up. An almost imperceptible shudder moved along his shoulder blades. "Crazy things. I'm saying crazy things." He stood, walked to the edge of the hill and looked out over the sea. Minutes passed. In a daze, Rebecca rose. She absently brushed a few crumbs from the blanket and slowly began to gather the picnic dishes and place them back in the basket. *What had happened? My God....*

At last Nick returned. "I can see the ferry coming back across the water," he announced. "I think we should go. I have to meet Noel at seven to go over some last-minute details about the show and...."

Rebecca just looked at him.

"Becca, *cara*," he began quietly, "what I said before...."

"What?" she asked. "Are you going to take it all back now? All the wonderful things?"

"No." He covered her hands, poised on the handle of the basket, with his own. "I take back nothing. I meant everything I said. But...."

"But...."

"I don't want to mislead you."

Rebecca shot him a fiery look.

"You are such a tender creature," he said. "And I am a hardened old bachelor with a heart like a barnacle, yet you totally unhinge me with your freshness and your sweetness. But Becca! You are so young. What do you know about love?"

"Plenty," she told him.

"Plenty..." he echoed. "You know nothing. Nothing. And it's such a crazy game. And at the moment, not one I'm sure we should play. Love comes and you think it's forever, and in your excitement you stumble headlong into the full catastrophe. Jealousy, betrayal, possessiveness, lust, sentimentality. And then suddenly it's over. It's vanished. And the loss is devastating."

She looked him squarely in the eye. "Who are you trying to protect? Me? Or you?"

He was taken aback. "Both of us." Then he stood

and attempted to regain his old voice. "Forgive me, Becca, I've spoken out of turn. I'm full of the sun and the champagne and the nearness of you and what I said earlier. . . ."

"Don't you dare apologize," she threatened, "for paying me a compliment." She impulsively threw her arms around him and drew him close. "I've had a wonderful day and I will not allow you to spoil it by apologizing." Her voice was husky with intensity.

She felt his surprise; then he gently returned the embrace. She heard him breathe into her hair. "You are the most astonishing girl."

"And I think you're all wrong about love," she told him. "It's none of those things you said. That's just some charade you've mistaken for love."

Now he laughed softly. "All right, you tell me."

"Real love is something you hold in your heart. And it never changes. It's part of who you are—"

"*Cara*, everything changes!"

"You're wrong!"

"Becca—" she could still hear the conflict of doubt and desire in his voice "—I don't want to argue. I just. . . ."

"What *do* you want?"

The look in his eyes was so sad. "To kiss you. Once more before we go."

BY THE FOLLOWING MORNING, a new crisis had arisen at the theater, and it took precedence over everything else. The actor playing the sizable role of Friar Laurence had fallen down his basement stairs the night before, breaking his ankle in two places. There was no way, the doctor claimed, that his sixty-year-old patient would be able to finish rehearsals and open in the play on Wednesday night. Nick wore a haggard look, as if he had not slept very much, when he advised the company of the situation at the ten o'clock rehearsal. "For the time being, Harry Moss will be standing in for the friar," he announced, "until we can make other arrangements. If worse comes to worst, I'll play the part myself, though I hope that won't be necessary.''

''Poor Nick,'' Chris whispered to Rebecca. ''Last week he lost the understudy. This week he loses the actor. Two days before the opening.''

''What a mess,'' she agreed. ''Just when everything was starting to pull together. What do you think will happen?''

''I don't know.'' He shrugged, then gave her a sly look out of the corner of his eye. ''Do you think perhaps Evany is ready to step into the part?''

''Hush!'' She laughed. ''This is serious.''

''I bet she is,'' Chris continued mischievously. ''I bet she's warming up in the alley. I bet she pushed him down the stairs.''

''Don't be silly. Evany is not interested in playing a monk!''

''I don't know,'' he countered. ''It's a bigger part.''

''The only part Evany is interested in is mine. And I plan to open in this show no matter what. Broken ankles, fevers, whatever. Nothing's going to stop me.''

''Well, I'm glad to see that you've developed a little fighting spirit,'' he said, congratulating her.

''I'm learning.'' She grinned.

As it happened, Chris did have a solution for the situation. At lunch he arranged a meeting between Nick, Noel and his father, who had arrived less than twenty-four hours earlier, expecting only to visit with his son and to sit with the rest of the audience on opening night. A certain amount of fervent cross-convincing and cajoling and conferring took place over pastrami sandwiches in Noel's office. When the actors reassembled on the mountain at two o'clock, it was announced that Ben Matheson would be taking over the role of Friar Laurence.

The man who stood up and introduced himself to the company was charming and silver-haired. He had acted the part before, he told them, and would do his best to catch up fast. He asked for their indulgence and was welcomed with a hearty round of applause. Most of the younger actors had grown up watching him preside over "Our House" and were intrigued to be working with their childhood hero. Rebecca took in the silver hair and the heavily lined face and realized that she knew something that almost no one else was aware of. This was a big moment in Ben Matheson's life. A kind of comeback—the first time he had ventured onto a stage in six years. He was taking a courageous step. He was coming out of seclusion.

He applied himself to the task at hand with a winning enthusiasm. Only Rebecca was aware that his hand shook slightly when he held the script. By the final dress rehearsal on Tuesday, he knew most of the lines, though he sometimes had to stop and think and pull them out of the air—as if the old Friar had momentarily become absentminded. Rebecca felt her own concentration double. *Please let him make it through,* she whispered in a prayer under her breath. *Let us all make it through.*

That night, the heavens responded by raining sporadically during the fourth act. In act 5, the rain stopped and a skunk wandered out of the woods and briefly onto the stage. She caught a glimpse of Nick sitting with his head in his hand, shaking it from side to side, as if he couldn't quite believe all the difficulties, large and small, that had descended upon his production at the eleventh hour.

When they were done at last, when they had received their notes and a rallying speech from Nick encouraging them to pull together and rise above all the distractions and upheavals, everyone departed wearily for home, feeling hopeful but not at all certain of the next day's outcome. Would everything go smoothly on opening night? Would the weather hold? Would the animals stay in the woods and leave the stage to the actors? Were they ready for an audience? Would the show hold? Would it sink? Would it be a hit?

"We're all too close to it," Gabe Daniels remarked to her as she was giving him a lift back into Sausalito. "We're too involved. We've lost our perspective. It could be great or it could be not-so-great. None of us can tell anymore. But, you know what they say...."

"What do they say?"

"Old theater superstition: if you have a rocky dress rehearsal, you'll have a good opening."

Rebecca laughed. "Well, in that case we should have a spectacular opening. Tonight couldn't have been much worse. That skunk was the last straw."

"I think we're going to be okay," he told her as he climbed out of the VW and bade her good night. "I consulted one of my astrology books and the stars are moving into a very favorable position. Fortune just may smile upon Shakespeare Bay tomorrow night."

"I hope you're right."

Would fortune smile upon her as well, she wondered as she drove home alone. Would it smile upon that innermost wish held secret in her heart? When the play officially opened, Nick Corelli's job was done. The actors were contracted to stay until *Romeo and Juliet* closed on September 3, but after tomorrow night Nick was free to go and do whatever he pleased.

Close as she had felt to him during that idyllic picnic two days ago—was it only two days ago?—she had no idea what his future plans were. In twenty-four hours, he might be gone forever.

CHAPTER EIGHT

REBECCA STOOD ON THE EDGE of the stage and stared up at the empty rows of stone seats. In just two hours, she reflected, they would be filled to capacity. In two hours, an expectant opening-night audience would be sitting out there, chatting, rustling their programs, waiting for the show to begin. Adam would be there, next to Maggie Byrne, who had invited him. And next to Maggie, Noel Rusk. And all around them, hundreds of people she didn't know and had never met, but who nevertheless would be sharing one of the more important evenings of her life. Her debut as a professional actress.

She caught her breath and listened to her heart knock against her breastbone. There was the old stage fright again, no doubt about it. She pressed her hand against her chest as a strange little hiccupy sound escaped her. The only other time she had felt stage fright so strongly was the day she had auditioned for the role. Was it only a month ago? Impossible. So much had happened. In the past month, she felt as if she had experienced more than in the previous ten years of her life. Nick Corelli had taken a coltish, independently spirited girl and turned her into a disciplined performer. And in the process she had lost her heart to him. The shy Mendocino tomboy had been transformed into someone new.

Only a month. It was hard to believe. Exactly one month ago, they had stood nose to nose, battling over a few square feet of asphalt. He had called her an idiot and she had called him an idiot. Then she had had to swallow her pride and knock herself out to win the role.

Today, everything had come full circle. *I asked for this,* she told her quaking self. *And I got my wish. Now I have to deliver the performance.* She wiped her perspiring hands against the legs of her jeans and looked again at the empty seats. This would not be some college crowd, full of doting parents and approving friends. These would be knowledgeable, seasoned theatergoers and a sprinkling of critics, waiting to measure her against other Juliets. She took a deep breath and raised herself to her full height, stretching out her arms as if to encompass the audience. Finding her voice, she spoke aloud the first lines that came into her head—"'Thou knowst the mask of night is on my face'"—and listened to them resonate against the stone. Her knees were shaking.

"What is this?" asked a voice behind her. "Some kind of bizarre ritual? Are you propitiating the gods of the theater or what?" It was Nick. He studied her suppliant posture with a bemused smile.

"Yes," she said over her shoulder. "I'm offering up my fear."

He laughed. "Do you have a little touch of nerves, Becca?"

"A touch?" she retorted. "I am fighting a deep primordial urge to take the next bus out of town! If I leave now, I could be in Nevada by the time the curtain goes up."

"Okay," he told her. "Go ahead."

She turned and looked at him in disbelief.

He was poker-faced. "I know Evany has been waiting a long time for an opportunity like this," he continued. "She'll probably be willing to pay for your ticket to Nevada. And from what I saw the other night, she'll give the part her best shot. I'm not worried. So go ahead. Don't let us keep you if you'd really rather be somewhere else."

"You skunk." She placed her hands on her hips and regarded him with a fierce look in her eye.

"I'm not a skunk." He shrugged. "I'm just trying

to help you out of your dilemma. That's what a good director is for, isn't it? To be of service to his actors. Now, can I drive you to the bus station?''

"I'm not going anywhere! I'm staying right here! No one else is going to play my role. Not Evany. Not anyone.''

"Ohhh..." he murmured. "You don't want to leave?''

"Of course not."

"I guess I misunderstood you," he apologized, his tone now maddeningly facetious. "Tell me, who do you think *should* play the role?''

"Me," she fumed. "I should play the role.''

"You?" He considered the possibility as if it had never occurred to him before. "Well, I don't know.... Do you think you're good enough? Do you think you can pull it off? I wouldn't want you to embarrass us all—here on opening night....''

"I can play this role better than anyone else you know. You are not going to be embarrassed, Nick Corelli. You are going to be impressed." She glared at him challengingly.

"Good," he said lightly. "I'm glad we got that straight. I'm delighted to hear the determination in your voice. Nothing could please me more.''

When she saw the comically blithe expression on his face, she had to laugh. "You're such a devil. You knew I was joking about the bus.''

"Joking?" He raised his eyebrows. "You looked pretty serious to me. You were standing there, shaking and carrying on about leaving town. I heard you talking yourself out of a performance. I heard you getting all wrapped up in your fear.''

"Oh, come on," she fussed. "Haven't you ever had stage fright?''

"You mustn't think of it as stage fright," he told her seriously.

"Then how do you suggest I interpret it?''

"As excitement.''

"What?"

"When you feel yourself trembling and your heart beating fast, you must say to yourself, 'Oh, look how excited I am to be here. I have such an appetite for my work. I love to act and here I am in a theater! What could be more perfect?' And then you take all that emotion and energy surging through you and you channel it right into your work."

"Ah...." She smiled. The idea made wonderful sense.

"Sure," he said. "You can think of it as fear and make it your enemy and try to conquer it. Or you can think of it as excitement and welcome it and make it work for you."

"Thank you." She reached out and clasped his hand. "Thank you. I think you just saved my life. Thank you. *Grazie.*"

"*Prego.*" He put his arm around her and gently kissed the top of her head. He smelled of cologne and she noted for the first time that he was dressed for the opening in a fine cotton shirt and a tie and tweed jacket. "Well, I've got to be off," he said. "I'll look for you at Noel's party after the show. I have something important to tell you. But for now, just remember one thing...."

"What's that?"

"It's supposed to be fun." He grinned. "Have a wonderful time out there."

SHE WAS SITTING in front of her makeup table, applying a thin coat of eyeliner, when she was startled by a rat-a-tat-tat at the door. "Come in," she called, wrapping the dressing gown closely about her. It was Tommy B., the boy who had served as gofer during rehearsals, arriving with an armload of flowers.

"Didn't mean to spook you," he said sheepishly, lugging the various bouquets and vases into the room.

"Oh, don't mind me." She laughed. "I'm just nervous...I mean excited...about tonight."

"Yeah, well, break a leg," he told her. "Most of these are for you."

When he had gone, she tore into the wrappings and accompanying envelopes with all the greedy relish of a five-year-old at her first big birthday party. Adam had sent wild flowers and a scrawled note that read, "Good luck, Sis." Rebecca's eyes grew moist. He was so dear; he'd probably gone out on the ranch and picked them himself; and he had no idea that theater superstition forbade anyone wishing an actor "good luck" before a show. Tommy B.'s salute had been the appropriate one.

From her leading man, there was a perky pot of violets and a quote from the play. "She doth teach the torches to burn bright" was Romeo's line upon first glimpsing Juliet, and Chris had inscribed it upon a card for her. Noel, bless his magnanimous heart, had sent the traditional dozen, long-stemmed red roses. And Maggie's best wishes clung to a vase stuffed with jonquils.

When Rebecca had arranged the bouquets around the sides of her dressing table, feeling very giddy and rich in friendship, she noticed a florist's box she had overlooked in her preoccupation with the more splashy of her presents. Lifting off the lid, she found herself gazing at an enormous white orchid, so exotic and so fragile that it almost seemed to quiver within the confines of the box. On a card, stuck in the side, was a single initial—*N*. No message, just *N*. She picked up the blossom and held it next to her face. It was an angel's breath. The dressing-room mirror told her exactly what to do with it. She'd wear it in her hair to the party Noel was hosting after the show. That way, Nick would see it when he came to tell her... what? What?

Just then, Sasha Costantine and Evany Pace arrived to share the dressing room, both of them full of laughter and giggles and high excitement. Rebecca quietly slipped the box into the little refrigerator that had been provided for the actresses and busied herself with opening a bottle of apple juice. The other two women greeted her effusively, apparently as keyed-up as she was over the coming event. They paused to admire her flowers before rushing over to see what awaited them on their own makeup tables. When Evany made a huge fuss over a bouquet of assorted blossoms she had received from Nick—identical to Sasha's, as it turned out—Rebecca, for once, did not envy her at all.

By eight twenty-five she was as ready as she would ever be. She stood in the waiting area in back of the set and reminded herself again how excited—not frightened—she was to be there. Her long dark hair was pulled back into a single thick braid, interlaced with ribbons and pearls. The spectacular rose-colored gown, Maggie's masterpiece, fit her like a dream. "You look wonderful," Chris whispered as he caught her by the waist and planted a good-luck kiss on her cheek.

"Ditto. Ditto," said Gabe as he collected his friend and hauled him off to the side entrance to await the opening scene.

"Break a leg, fellows," she called after them sotto voce and then, remembering the former Friar Laurence's unfortunate accident, wondered if the epithet was as harmless as it seemed.

Suddenly she heard the audience grow quiet. The sound of a thousand voices and a thousand rattling programs faded to a hush. The lights were going down. She closed her eyes and offered up a silent prayer. *Let it go well. Let it not rain. Let there be no skunks. Let Ben Matheson remember his lines. And let me do the best of which I am capable.* Then the music sounded, a flurry of silver-voiced trumpets in the cool night. The play had begun.

WHEN SHE MADE her first entrance, she could tell that things were going very well indeed. The audience was alert and responsive. They laughed over the byplay be-

tween Juliet and her bawdy nurse and seemed suitably
amused by Evany as the pretentious Lady Capulet. By
the ballroom scene, they were clearly enraptured. The
actors had all sensed the warmth of the response they
were receiving, and it functioned as so much fuel to
the fire. The play burst into full and joyous flame.
Scenes began to fly. Chris and Rebecca finished the
balcony duet to a thunderous round of applause.

In the second half, the play darkened into tragedy.
Gabe Daniels died a spectacular death as Mercutio
and was carried off in a wash of fake blood. Rebecca
made a face when she saw him backstage, gory and
begrimed, but he only winked at her and mouthed the
words, "Karo Syrup."

Then it was her turn again. She gave herself over to
the stormy emotions demanded of her, playing a difficult scene with Ben Matheson for all it was worth.
He was holding his own. He faltered once during a
long speech but soon recovered, making the audience
believe that the old friar had been too overcome to
speak for a moment. *It's going so well,* Rebecca
thought to herself. *No accidents. Nothing amiss.*

Act 5 scene 3 rolled around before they knew it. The
show was almost over. She took her place upon the
funeral bier in the dim-lit tomb. Chris entered, wept
over her limp form and downed his cup of poison. The
audience was breathless, straining silently on the edge
of their seats.

But when it came time for her to wake, to discover
his body and then take her own life with the dagger
from his belt... she could not find the wretched instrument! There was no dagger. It simply wasn't
there. She felt the panic begin in her heart and spread
rapidly throughout her system. *There was no dagger.*
How could she die when there was no dagger to stab
herself with? The audience waited patiently, unaware
as yet that anything had gone wrong.

She thought of Nick, sitting in the third row, wondering why she didn't simply get on with it. She

thought of the twenty other actors, waiting backstage to make a final entrance. How could she let them all down? She improvised a bit of business that allowed her to look on each side of the bier to see if, perhaps, the knife had fallen on the floor by mistake. It wasn't there.

How can this be, she asked herself. This was an actor's nightmare and it was happening...to her. She was caught before hundreds of people with egg on her face. She wished the floor would open and mercifully swallow her.

Now the audience was beginning to stir. She thought she could hear a few silibant whispers floating on the night air. "What's she doing, Jack?" "I don't know, Mabel." A fresh tear rolled down her cheek. It was just too awful. She tried frantically to think of other ways to die. Perhaps Juliet could slip and break her neck. Or have a heart attack? No, no, that was no good. Tomorrow, all the reviews would jeer: "New interpretation of old classic—Juliet dies of cardiac arrest." At last, she threw herself upon Chris's prostrate form and wept in good earnest. She simply did not know what else to do. "It's underneath me," she heard him whisper. "I'm lying on it."

She cradled his supposedly dead body in her arms and rocked him as if overcome with grief. This allowed her to free the knife at last. With a moan of relief, she grasped it in one hand, delivered her final lines and plunged it into the soft padding of her costume. And it was over. The other actors came scurrying on, and after a few speeches the play was done.

Moments later, she was taking a curtain call, radiant and elated as she had ever been. The applause rolled in like a huge wave. She smiled and curtsied, feeling as if she had been lifted from purgatory into the arms of grace.

"YOU WERE WONDERFUL, my dear, just wonderful!" Noel told her later when she arrived at the party. "We really didn't know what was going on there at the end, but we were absolutely riveted. I thought you'd become inspired and decided to play Juliet a little crazed. Such an interesting idea...."

"I was crazed." She laughed. In retrospect, it was all beginning to seem rather funny. She accepted a glass of white wine from a passing waiter and sipped it gratefully.

"Well," he said with a sigh, "when Chris told me about the dagger, I was fit to be tied. I think you handled the whole thing quite well."

"I'm just relieved that I didn't embarrass all of you."

"Embarrass...!" He made a tasking sound. "My dear, you are a very special young actress—in case you are unaware of that fact. Not only are you pretty but you can play all of the more difficult ingenue roles. You are a producer's godsend. Now, there's something I want to talk to you about...." He put an arm around her shoulders and took her confidentially to one side.

Rebecca was taken aback by this unexpected praise. It was true, she had worked very hard to rise to the challenge offered by the part, and she had, when taunted by Nick, made a few defensive boasts concerning her abilities. But she had never really thought of herself as anything more than a fledgling trying desperately to fly.

"I'm planning to mount a production of *Hamlet* in San Francisco this fall," Noel continued. "I'm going to direct it myself and I want Chris to play Hamlet and Ben Matheson to play the king. We'll rehearse at Shakespeare Bay and open at a theater in the city in late October. What do you think? Would you be interested in doing Ophelia?"

"Noel—" she choked, almost spilling her wine "—do you mean it?"

"Of course I mean it." He drew himself up to his full, imperial six-foot-two. "Do I look like a joker? Now, I know it's still a ways off and you don't have to commit yourself right now. Just think about it."

"I will," she murmured.

"Good." He smiled and clicked her glass with his own. "Now, go and have some fun. Dance with some of the young men. I'm sure you don't want to stand here all night, talking to an old coot like me."

Before she could protest, a new flood of guests appeared at the door and Noel moved to welcome them. Rebecca wandered into the living room of his spacious home, mulling over the offer he had just made her. Ophelia was a marvelous part. She had not really stopped to think where her next job might come from, and here it had just fallen into her lap. Everything was happening so fast.

The room was filled with people, many of whom she knew from Shakespeare Bay, but there were an equal number she didn't recognize. Friends of Noel's, patrons of the theater, she supposed; they were an elegant crew. From the corner came the sound of a piano tinkling out an old Cole Porter melody. A svelte young woman leaned against the side of Noel's baby grand, singing along in a low whiskey-dark voice. Rebecca smiled. Apparently her godfather had engaged a singer and a pianist to entertain his guests. Trust Noel to do things with class.

She caught a glimpse of herself in a mirror and was glad she'd opted to wear a simple but stylishly cut silk dress, the newest addition to her wardrobe. It was a dusty pink and the uneven hemline wafted around her legs in a series of fluttering panels. And, in her hair, the white orchid. She looked around the room for Nick and spotted him at last, deep in conversation with Maggie and Adam. Rebecca had seen Nick briefly after the performance, when he had come backstage to bestow hugs and bravos upon the cast, but she was still in mystery as to what he was waiting to discuss with her. Did it concern his future plans, since as of this evening he was no longer bound to Shakespeare Bay? She caught sight of him now, talking excitedly as he raked his dark hair back off his brow in a characteristically volatile gesture. A warm ache spread through her chest. She hardly dared to think about the future.

"Here's our Juliet!" a new voice proclaimed above the noise of the party. Rebecca turned to see a chubby bald-headed man moving toward her. "I'm Howard Boggs from the Second Stage in Seattle," he said as he pumped her hand enthusiastically. "I was at the performance tonight and I so enjoyed your work, Miss Yates. You were a breath of fresh air."

Rebecca ducked her head shyly but managed to utter a polite thank-you. Taking compliments was still not her forte.

"You know what they always say about Juliet. . ." he continued jovially.

"What do they say?"

"Most actresses who look the part are too inexperienced to play it. And by the time an actress has developed the capacity to act it properly, she's already too old for the role. But you. . . you were the exception."

"Thank you," she said again. Suddenly, she sensed another presence at her elbow. It was Nick.

"Hello, Howard," he greeted the beaming Mr. Boggs. "I've come to steal Rebecca away from you. She's promised me this dance," he lied with a mischievous twinkle in his eye.

"You're the man of the hour, Nick," Howard Boggs conceded. "I was just about to tell Miss Yates that I hope she'll come up to Seattle sometime and work with us at Second Stage. We could use an ingenue of her caliber." He shook Rebecca's hand again. "Let's keep in touch," he told her. "Noel will give you my business address."

"Who was that man?" she asked Nick when he had swept her out the French doors onto a patio where a number of couples were dancing cheek to cheek to the piano player's old-fashioned repertoire. The night was balmy. She slipped easily into his arms.

"He's the artistic director of Second Stage. It's a good theater. You should take him up on his offer. Keep in touch. He could give you a job someday."

"Oh," she said. "Well, that would mean moving to Seattle, I suppose."

"For the run of your contract," Nick said. "Two months, three months, four months; it depends on whether or not they hire you for more than one show."

"I see."

He laughed when he saw the look of consternation on her face. "You've chosen a very nomadic profession, my dear. It's a Gypsy's life. You're always on the move. Lots of rented apartments. New cities. New faces. New friends. Then, just when you've got your bearings, bingo, everything changes again."

"I don't know if I like the sound of that."

"You'll learn to like it. You must. . . if this is really what you want to do. It can be exciting. In the past year, I've spent five months in New York, a month and a half in London, two months in Italy, two months in Stratford, Ontario, a month here and two weeks—" he chuckled "—in my farmhouse in the country outside Rome." He pulled her close and spun her around the floor. "What is that perfume you're wearing?" he growled into her ear. "It's driving me absolutely crazy."

"I don't think I have on any perfume," she told him. "I was in such a hurry after the show. Maybe it's the orchid."

"I don't think so." He grinned. "It must be your own sweet self."

"Are you trying to sweet-talk me, Nick Corelli?"

"Yeah," he crooned into her hair. "How am I doing?"

The sheer proximity of him was having its usual effect upon her. "Not bad," she answered in what she hoped was a breezy tone.

"Come on." He took her hand and led her toward a

footpath that wound down into Noel's garden. "Let's take a walk."

The piano and the chatter from the party faded to a distant murmur, and the flowering trees and bushes shed their fragrance into the warm dark air. A lone cricket sang his love song from the grass. The night had suddenly turned magical. They wandered by a pool stocked with goldfish, the creatures' bright backs catching and reflecting the light from the moon. Nick lifted her hand and buried a kiss in its palm. "How are you, Becca?" he asked. "Tired? That was quite a performance you turned in tonight."

"It's crazy," she said, instantly rattled by the kiss. "In one way, I'm bone tired. I'm exhausted. But in another I'm wide awake. I have lots of energy. I could stay up all night." She laughed, intoxicated as much by his presence as by the residue of her performance. Then she broke away from him, stepped up onto the brick-lined rim of the fishpond and walked around it, balancing with both arms held out at her sides.

"I know how you feel," he said. "Acting is an enormous rush. Your adrenaline soars."

"It's wonderful."

"It is," he agreed. "But please. Don't get carried away and fall into the pond."

"I'm not going to fall," she insisted merrily. "Besides, it's only two feet deep."

"Nonetheless," he scolded, "you're making me very nervous in those high heels. Come on, put your hands on my shoulders. I'll help you down."

At that very instant, as if by the power of his suggestion, her heel stuck in a chink in the brick, throwing her off balance. She wavered wildly for a moment before Nick caught her by the waist. She reached out for him and suddenly she was in his arms. He held her as she slid helplessly down the front of his body. She was instantly aflame. She heard him sigh. Her feet touched the ground at last. His fingers entangled themselves in her hair and his mouth found hers in a hungry kiss.

She was lost. The love she felt for him rose up inside and overwhelmed her. She forgot everything—the play, the party, the people inside. There was only Nick. She buried her hands in his hair and held his head as he covered her face and neck in soft burning kisses. When he unbuttoned the front of her dress and slid his hand inside the silk bodice, cupping her breast in his palm, she made no protest.

There was no time. His mouth sought hers once more in a deep searching kiss. His tongue was warm and sweet and infinitely adroit. He was an artist in more ways than one. She sank against him with a rapturous, drowning sensation. Her consciousness faded from indigo to black.

When they drew apart at last, both of them breathless and more than a little shaky with the passion that had claimed them so abruptly, Nick was the first to find his voice again. "Becca...Becca..." he whispered hoarsely, stroking her cheek with his fingers. "I wish...."

"What?" she asked when he hesitated and seemed to grope for the next words. "What do you wish?"

He sighed, raking the hair back from his forehead in a gesture of frustration. "I wish...there was more time. I wish I didn't have to leave so soon...."

From the depths of her arousal, she felt a high cold note of alarm begin to sound. She sat down on the edge of the fishpond and tried to sound calm. "Leave? Where are you going?"

"Well, my job here is finished," he began.

"Yes. Yes, I know. I mean, I knew...that after tonight...you would be...."

"Unemployed." He completed the sentence for her, trying to make a little joke of it. "My contract is up. And the fact is...I've been offered another project that begins almost immediately."

"Oh," she said hollowly. "Well, congratulations. That's great. What is it?"

"It's a new play by an Italian playwright. An old

friend of mine is planning to produce it and sent me the script only a few days ago to see if I would be interested in directing. It's a marvelous story, the best original material I've come across in years." She could hear the enthusiasm in his voice. "As soon as I read it, I knew I had to do it. This will be the world premiere."

"I see. Where? What theater?"

"Rome," he replied. "Years ago, when I was first starting out, I worked with a theater there that was headed by a woman named Francesca Cini."

"I've heard of her." Rebecca was beginning to feel ill.

"Yes, well, Francesca has always been a great innovator, a great developer of new talent. She discovered this playwright and was considering directing the piece herself. But she's so involved now with the administration of the theater that she decided to offer the job to me."

"How nice of her."

"And I couldn't say no. The play is just too good." His eyes sparkled. "Francesca knew it would be my cup of tea," he said with a laugh, as if at some private joke. "We parted company years ago and I swore I'd never work with her again, but I'm sure she realized that I couldn't possibly turn down something like this."

He continued to ramble on about the play, outlining the plot and mentioning some of his own ideas concerning it, but Rebecca was no longer able to take in what he was saying. She was fairly sick with emotion. Loss, grief, rage, pain raced through her system in swift succession. He was leaving. He would soon be gone. She would probably never see him again. *Well, what did you expect,* she asked herself angrily. *Just what did you expect? Did you think he was going to hang around forever just to be with you? Did you think he was going to carry you off on a white horse? You did, didn't you? Fool.* She could feel the tears beginning to well, but she fiercely choked them back. She would not disgrace herself any further by crying over his departure. He had told her at the beginning that he was a nomad, that he was married to his work. Francesca would have to be content with second place in his affections—if she succeeded in luring him back into her life. Women were the mistresses. Theater was the bride.

"We'll start work immediately," he was saying, "and open the first of September." His eyes swept over her face. He paused for a moment as if he were waiting for some response from her. Rebecca was too numb to speak. Nick registered an odd look of disappointment before outlining the rest of his plans.

Why had she ever thought she might have mattered to him? Because of the way he kissed her? Because he'd taken her on a picnic and talked about tenderness? Because he'd once confessed to being jealous of Chris Matheson? It had been a dalliance on his part, nothing more than a dalliance. He had dallied first with Evany and then with her. And maybe with a few others she knew nothing about. He was in a strange city. He was alone. He was killing time.

"Becca?" He was calling her name. She snapped back to attention.

"Yes?"

"Are you listening? *Cara*, I want to know what you think."

"I think you're a fine director." Her voice was flat, but she rallied herself to pay him the only honest compliment she could. "I'm sure you'll have a great success."

"Grazie." He reached for her hand and kissed the back of it. "Thank you...but I guess I'm fishing for something a little more personal...."

"What do you mean?"

His laugh was low, self-deprecating. He studied the contours of her fingers for a moment. "I want to know how you feel about what I've been saying, *cara*.

I want to hear how sorry you are that I have to go.''

"When are you leaving?" she asked fuzzily.

"Tomorrow morning."

She felt as if her heart had turned to stone. The *ego* of the man. He cared nothing for her—that was clear. He was leaving the next day. He only wanted the gratification of knowing he had made an impression. In a kind of haze, she took her hand back and began rebuttoning the front of her dress. "Becca," he murmured, attempting to stop her, but she shook his hand off and rose to her feet.

"I'm sure everyone will miss you, Nick. Rest assured." She turned to go.

"Not everyone. You! Becca! Wait. Where are you going?"

"Back inside," she told him. "It's late. The party will be over soon. I've hardly spoken to my brother all evening."

"Don't go," he said. "Not yet. I haven't finished. . . .''

"Haven't you?" she asked, unable to suppress the note of anger in her voice. "Haven't you finished, Nick? I know I have."

He seemed somewhat taken aback by this. He frowned. "I want to give you my address in Rome," he said.

She looked at him blankly. "Whatever for?"

"I thought," he said testily, beginning to pick up her tone, "that you might write to me."

"I doubt I'll have time," she retorted. "I'm going to be awfully busy. You see, I've had some good news, too. Noel's offered me a part in his upcoming production of *Hamlet*. Plus there's still *Romeo and Juliet* every evening. . . .''

"Congratulations." He scowled. "You'll make a wonderful Ophelia."

"Thanks," she replied, glad she had at least one ace to toss upon the table to show that she, too, had places to go and commitments to keep. "It's exciting, isn't it? Chris is going to be Hamlet and Ben Matheson's in it, too.''

"Cozy."

She smoothed back her hair, which was disheveled by his embrace. The orchid came loose and fell at her feet. When she picked it up, she saw that it had been broken and had begun to turn brown. "Oh," she said softly, feeling the tears well in her eyes once more, "it was so lovely."

"I thought so." His voice tore at her.

"Well," she said with a shrug, tossing the flower into the fishpond where it spun forlornly before sinking beneath the surface. "Nothing lasts forever. Everything changes. Isn't that what you said?"

"Did I?"

"You did," she reminded him.

"Rebecca—" he caught the hem of her skirt between his fingers "—when you kissed me a little while ago...."

"I meant it about as much as you did. It was fun, that's all. Count it as a goodbye kiss." A tear spilled down her cheek and she brushed it away quickly before he looked up into her face once more. "Now, for heaven's sake, Nick, let go of my dress before you tear it."

He refused to do so.

"What do you want?" she demanded.

He said nothing.

"What is it? Is there anything else we have to discuss? Because I really have to be going."

"No," he said at last, his voice tight. "There's nothing you and I have to discuss. It's all been said. Except this. *Arrivederci.*"

"Goodbye," she murmured.

JUST AS SHE REACHED the steps to the patio, alone and half-blinded by tears, she heard a huge cheer go up inside the house. The piano tinkled out the opening bars of "For He's a Jolly Good Fellow" and then someone began to make a speech. Rebecca stepped through the open French doors and found herself on the periphery of a circle of well-wishers who now filled the living room. In the center were Maggie and Adam, champagne glasses aloft, their arms encircling each other's waists.

"The wedding's September 4 at Adam's place in Mendocino," Maggie was telling the assembled company, a big trembly smile on her face. "And you're all invited."

A second cheer greeted them. Sasha Constantine and Noel simultaneously rushed forward to embrace Maggie. Adam caught his sister's eye and, before she could quite register what was happening, he pulled her to him in a big bear hug.

"Adam!" she stammered. "Did I hear right? Are you...?"

"Yep." He grinned his wide cowboy grin. "Getting married. Maggie finally said yes. I had to chase her and chase her, but she finally said yes. Hey now, don't cry, baby, this is a happy occasion—"

"Becca!" Maggie swooped down upon her, laughing and hugging her and kissing her on the cheek. "I'm sorry we didn't tell you before, but we wanted to surprise everybody. You're not mad, are you? What are you crying for? Now, stop it or I'll cry too."

"We thought we'd have the ceremony out in the south pasture at the ranch," Adam put in. "Beneath one of those big old oak trees you used to like to climb. Won't that be nice? An outdoor wedding? The horses can even come if they want to—"

"They can not," Maggie said, dabbing her eyes with the handkerchief from his coat pocket. "I'm not having any horses upstaging me at my wedding. Now come on, Becca, don't cry. You're spoiling your makeup, sugar. I'm going to need you, you know, to help me pull this thing off. I want you to be a bridesmaid. Here, let me dry your eyes with this hanky."

"We're real happy, baby sister. I love her a lot."

"We are, Becca. I'm going to take good care of your brother. He's the only man for me."

"Dammit," Adam growled as the two women fell into each other's arms and rocked back and forth, each sobbing for her own separate reasons, one out of happiness, the other from loss. "A couple of crybabies, that's what you are."

CHAPTER NINE

THE REVIEWS OF THE SHOW were uniformly good. The first appeared in one of the San Francisco papers on the same day Nick left for Rome. He missed seeing it by only a few hours. Gabe dutifully cut it out and mailed it to him, enclosed in a greeting card that the cast was invited to sign. Rebecca scribbled her name at the bottom. It would have looked funny if she had refused. Besides, she really did have a lot to thank him for.

Her performance had been praised as "passionate and sure...exhibiting both skill and a remarkable depth of feeling. Miss Yates is tender, innocent, ferocious and wise. What more could we ask for in any Juliet?" It was largely due to Nick's guidance, she admitted to herself, that she had managed to come off so well in her first professional role. It was due to all those hours he had spent coaxing and pushing and honing her until she got it right. His genius was present in every move she made.

If he was present in her performance, he was rarely absent in her offstage thoughts, much as she would have wished it otherwise. His face was the first image that floated into her consciousness when she woke each morning. The echo of his laugh followed her around all day, even though she knew he was thousands of miles away. When she fell asleep at night, she inevitably slipped into his phantom embrace.

"It's so strange," she told Samcat, who had taken to lugging the kittens into Rebecca's bed each night. "Here I am playing the great romantic heroine of all time. I get flowers, I get applause, I even get a little fan mail. But I'm so lonely I could curl up and die of it. The more I try to forget him, the more he's on my mind. The very act of trying to forget is somehow an act of remembering. I was better off when I didn't know what love was."

The days came and went. One performance followed another. Soon it was July. Then August. Chris Matheson dropped by late one afternoon, took a look at Samcat and her brood and announced that the time had come to have the christening party. "Those kittens are getting big," he told her. "If you don't give them away now, they'll soon be cats, and then no one will adopt them. You have to act now while they're still cute."

"I don't know." She hesitated. "Technically, they all belong to Perry."

"Perry is *not* going to thank you if he comes home next month and finds his houseboat overrun with six big pussycats. So. . . how about having the party this coming Monday night. The theater will be dark. We don't have a show to do that evening. Everyone will be able to come over, have a glass of wine and christen the kitten of their choice. If they christen it, they have to take it home. No returns."

It sounded like a good idea. Besides, it gave her something new to think about. She forgot Nick for three whole hours Monday afternoon while she and Chris shopped for cheeses and an array of good Napa Valley wines. They stocked Rebecca's kitchen and cut crepe-paper streamers, which the kittens chased across the floor, and waited for the first guests to arrive.

The party accomplished its purpose better than either of them had dared to hope. Approximately twenty-five people from Shakespeare Bay showed up to share the wine and play with the kittens. After a couple of rounds of charades, they were all in a generous, free-wheeling mood. Maggie led the way by scooping up the runt of the litter and christening it

"Romeo." This started a trend. Gabe and Sasha also adopted kittens, naming them after characters in the play. One of the stagehands took one as a present for his daughter. Rebecca was delighted. Only one lone kitten remained. But, try though they might, neither she nor Chris could convince anyone else to make a home for the last lump of fur curled up by Samcat's side.

"I'd take it," Evany told Rebecca at the end of the evening as she searched for her wrap among the bags and jackets piled high upon the bed, "but this new man I'm seeing is allergic to cats." She giggled. "He's absolutely divine and he's practically camped at my house. I can't have him sneezing all over me, now can I?"

"I suppose not," Rebecca agreed and then added, tongue-in-cheek, "Not if he's as *divine* as you say...."

"Well, of course, I don't mean *divine* in the sense that Nicky Corelli was *divine*," Evany continued in an airy rueful tone. "That would be going a bit far. But George is sufficiently divine to last me through the summer." She found her jacket and slipped it around her shoulders. "Which reminds me. Look what I came across today." She pulled a European fashion magazine out of her bag and flipped to a page she had earmarked.

There, next to a column filled with social gossip, was a picture of Nick, taken at some recent gala, arm in arm with a vivid dark-haired woman. "N. Corelli *e* F. Cini" the caption read. Rebecca felt her spirits, which had been relatively high all evening, suddenly drop to the sodden earth with a thud. "Not bad looking for an old dame," Evany commented. "She's got to be in her forties." Francesca looked neither old nor bad. She looked ageless. Regal. Handsome. "Oh, well—" Evany dropped the magazine on the bed "—no use crying over spilt milk, I always say. You keep the magazine. There's a great spread on fall clothes you may want to look at. I'm going home to George."

When the last guest had departed and she was alone again, Rebecca could not resist taking a second long look at the photograph, distressing though it was to her. "What am I?" she muttered irritably as she thumbed to the designated page. "A glutton for punishment?" Still she knew she could not throw the magazine away. Not just yet.

Nick smiled up at her, a perfect row of white teeth in the rough handsome face she knew so well. He looked elegant and rakish in the formal black and white of his evening clothes. Even in a photograph, an aura of restless energy was somehow visible. Francesca Cini, only slightly less striking than Sophia Loren, her contemporary, held his arm. His hand covered hers solicitously. Rebecca studied the other woman's face as if searching for a clue to her personality. She was Nick's female counterpart, no doubt about it. There was the same pride, the same intensity, the same boldness. Together, they were a matched pair of lions.

When Rebecca closed the magazine at last and lay down upon the bed, prepared for a good long cry, she was surprised to find she had no tears left. She was simply cried out. The hurt was still there, the sense of loss like a yawning hole in her chest. She was still angry with him—for pursuing her as ardently and yet as ambiguously as he had, leaving her hopelessly confused by his inconsistency. A kiss here, an evasion there, a breathless reconciliation, and then gone for good. It wasn't fair.

They had been so tender with each other. And so cruel. He had opened a whole new world that she didn't even know existed and then left her to live in it alone. She had prattled to him about love and then refused even to write to him. What sort of people were they, after all? Fickle? Creatures of constant change—as Nick had insisted?

She sighed, closed her eyes and listened to her heartbeat, to the rise and fall of her own breath. And then the understanding came to her. She loved him. Purely.

Completely. With or without his returning her love, she loved him. Beneath the anger and the jealousy and the waves of pain was a small steady flame that was love.

They had both been right. Some things changed. And some things remained ever the same.

THE NEXT DAY Chris had some unexpected news to share. His mother and sister had arrived in San Francisco and were planning to attend the performance that very night. He bustled around, finagling a pair of hitherto unavailable tickets in the center of the seventh row. Rebecca could see how excited he was by their visit. Although he didn't spell it out, she knew that tonight would be the first time in many years that the entire Matheson family had been assembled in one place.

The play went especially well that evening. Chris threw himself into the part with fresh enthusiasm. The other actors, many of whom had allowed themselves to become a trifle lazy after two months of doing the same show six times a week, caught his spirit and rose to the occasion. The audience responded with a standing ovation.

Rebecca was introduced to Nancy and Mia Matheson backstage after the performance by an ebullient Chris. Later she watched with pleasure as all four Mathesons left the amphitheater in a single car in search of a late-night supper. Ben Matheson had given his best performance to date, she reflected. He had looked so animated, almost robust. Perhaps that particular family saga had some happy chapters yet to come.

"I wouldn't be surprised," Maggie commented when Rebecca told her about the episode a few days later. "I hear Noel is trying to talk Nancy Matheson into joining the cast of *Hamlet*. He wants her to play the queen."

"You don't say!" Rebecca was perched on a stool in the kitchen of Maggie's houseboat, helping her future sister-in-law address a stack of wedding invitations. "Three Mathesons in one show. That would be quite a coup."

"Well, Noel's no dummy. Three Mathesons would be good for box office—in addition to their being excellent actors." Maggie crossed off another name from her long list, put down her pen and massaged the cramp in her right hand. If everyone accepted, there would be five hundred people convening at the Mendocino ranch on September 4.

"What about the costumes for *Hamlet*?" Rebecca asked. "Are you doing them?"

"Nope." Maggie grinned. "I'm going to be on my honeymoon. I don't plan to work for the next three months. I told Noel he'd have to get someone else to design this one." She laughed. "I'm turning over a new leaf. 'No thanks' is pretty strong language coming from a workaholic like me."

"But you're not giving up your career altogether, are you?"

"Oh, no! I couldn't do that. I love it too much. I'll do two or three shows a year." She picked up her pen and resumed her task. "I couldn't give up designing any more than Adam could give up his horses. And I'd never think of asking him to do that. I don't think you can begrudge someone the work they love. It wouldn't be fair. But you can make a few compromises. We talked it over. I'll do two or three shows instead of six and he'll agree to live in the house instead of the stables."

"You make it sound so simple."

"It isn't. But when you love someone, you work things out." She tossed an invitation onto the "done" stack and reached for another. "Good heavens, I hope all these people don't come! We'll never be able to feed them." Maggie sighed and studied her list. "Well, here's one who won't show up," she said brightly. "Nicky Corelli. But I'm going to send him an invitation anyhow, just for old times' sake." She scribbled a foreign address across the envelope. "I heard from him the other day, did I tell you?"

"No." Rebecca felt her cheeks begin to glow. She ducked her head and concentrated on the invitation she was addressing. "What'd he have to say?"

"Not a lot. It was only a postcard. His new show is about to open. He's real excited about it."

Rebecca smiled and nodded, unable to speak.

"So...if you want to copy down his address, go ahead," Maggie prompted in her pixie-light voice.

"Why would I want to do that?"

Maggie gave her a long squinty-eyed look. Then she placed both hands on her hips and took a deep breath. Rebecca could sense a lecture coming. "Because his show is about to open!" Maggie began. "Because it would be nice if you wrote him a note and wished him good luck! Because it would be a generous supportive thing to do!"

"I don't know if—"

"What's the matter with you, Becca? You know what it's like to undertake a big job and put in a lot of work and have all that pressure and attention on you. It's scary, isn't it? You know how important it is to have the support of your friends."

"Nick isn't scared—"

"He's a human being, isn't he? What do you think he is? The colossus of Rhodes, made out of stone? Tell me, wasn't he there helping you every inch of the way when you opened in *Romeo and Juliet*?" Maggie ran her hands through her short curly hair. "I'm sorry. I guess it's none of my business. I just thought you two had got kind of close when you were working together. I know he liked you. I thought you liked him."

"I do," Rebecca said hoarsely. Her throat had begun to cave in and she could scarcely breathe. "I'm crazy about him."

"Oh...." Maggie's voice resumed its normal register. "I see. So it's love, isn't it?"

Rebecca nodded her head, cheeks aflame.

"Hmm." Maggie made a little humming sound. "Does he know?"

"No! Well...I'm not sure. Maybe."

"Did you ever tell him?"

"No...I never could.... Besides, he doesn't love me...."

"Are you sure about that?"

"He's gone!" Rebecca sighed impatiently. "He's half a world away. He's with that Cini woman. He's—"

"Becca—" Maggie's voice was gentle but firm "—do me a favor, will you? Do yourself a favor. Copy down his address. Write him a note and tell him you wish him luck. That's all. You can't lose anything by doing that, now can you?"

"Well...."

Maggie smiled. "Pride is a good thing, I suppose, but not if you wind up choking to death on it. Look, you do what you want. Here's the address." She scribbled it onto a slip of paper and stuck it into Rebecca's pocket. "You do with it what you want."

In the end, she wound up following Maggie's suggestion. She wrote him a short note of four or five lines conveying her good wishes and dropped it into the mail before she had time to chicken out. It was a good letter, she told herself, and it was all true, every single word of it. She hadn't mooned and she hadn't begged. And besides, she'd probably never see him again.

THE MORNING OF SEPTEMBER 4 dawned fair and blue and warm. Rebecca was up at six. She gulped down a cup of tea, climbed into the rickety but still mobile VW and took off for Mendocino before the rest of the traffic had a chance to claim the road. The ranch was a three-hour drive from Sausalito and, once she arrived, there would be a hundred and one things to do. The food. The flowers. The music. Her dress. Maggie. Adam. Three hundred and fifty confirmed guests. And the ceremony scheduled to begin at four.

In a way, she welcomed the activity. *Romeo and Juliet* had closed the night before, amid tears and laughter and lots of hugs all around. She had been truly sorry to see it come to an end. It had been the focal point of her life for so many months—a minisociety populated by actors and stagehands, dressers and ushers, and the rest of the staff at Shakespeare Bay. Some would soon join the preparations for *Hamlet*. But many would not. It was the end of a chapter.

It was like saying goodbye to Nick a second time.

"Bless you, Becca, for getting here so early!" Maggie cried when the VW pulled into the driveway at last. "I'm afraid I'm never going to get everything done in time. I still have to hem my dress—would you believe it?—in addition to everything else."

Rebecca laughed at the sight of her friend, the bride-to-be, standing in the yard of the ranch house, tousle-haired and wild-eyed, dressed in a pair of cutoff jeans and one of Adam's old T-shirts. "I'm here to help," she told Maggie. "Just tell me where to begin."

"Well, let's see." Maggie stared at her fingers as if each one represented a separate herculean task. "Adam's down in the pasture with one of his friends. They've borrowed folding chairs from the church and they're busy setting them up. About noon, another man is arriving with a piano, no less, on the back of a flatbed truck, upon which he intends to plunk out the wedding march. I said it was foolhardy; but Adam insisted on live music. There's a fiddler coming, too. I think this is going to be more bluegrass than Mendelssohn, but why not? In the meantime, I've got a barrel of fresh-cut flowers and garlands and who-knows-what-all out on the back porch. Why don't you and I take it down to the pasture and start decorating the platform they've built? We'll worry about the food later on."

"Maggie," Rebecca teased. "Isn't it bad luck to see the groom before the wedding? Shouldn't you go take a nap or do your nails or read some poetry or something?''

"Are you kidding?" Maggie rolled her eyes. "This is a pioneer wedding. If I don't look good to him now, the dress and the bouquet won't make any difference. Come on, let's get moving."

They all worked hard and long, and by noon, when the piano arrived, the little makeshift wooden platform beneath the oak trees had been transformed into a woodland chapel. Adam paused to give his bride a sweaty kiss before hiking off to catch two curious ponies that had somehow found their way into the pasture. Rebecca assisted him in walking them back to the corral.

"How're you doing, big brother?" she asked playfully. "Are you nervous at all?"

"Nope," he told her solemnly. "I said I was going to marry her and I am."

Rebecca had to smile. Adam was approaching matrimony the same way he had approached everything else in his life. He simply set his mind to it and then he did it, with very little comment or second thought. He had been a dedicated bachelor and now, in one clean turn, he would become a dedicated husband. Maggie had known a good thing when she had seen it.

"I 'preciate you helping out," he drawled. "One day soon, it'll be your turn, Becca."

"Oh, I don't think I'm ever going to marry," she responded. "I'm going to live to be a very old actress, alone with my scrapbooks and a couple of poodle dogs."

Adam snorted. "Never say never. Look what happened to me."

By one o'clock a van arrived, bearing an array of tasty dishes from the kitchen of a local inn. "Please show them where to put everything, Becca," Maggie called from the living room where she sat cross-legged on the floor, hastily hemming her wedding gown. Rebecca obliged, directing traffic as best she could and wondering when she was going to find time to take a bath. Under the shade of the porch roof, Adam was icing down the champagne. The fiddler sat on the steps, tuning his instrument to the utter fascination of the ranch's old Irish setter.

Soon people began to arrive by twos and threes. The best man, a lifelong friend of Adam's, along with several other local pals who had volunteered to help host and usher, roared up in a series of Jeeps and pickup trucks. There were three dainty bridesmaids in a Mercedes from the city. Noel was on hand to give the bride away. The house was fairly bursting at the seams.

At last Rebecca managed to steal away to her room, shower hurriedly and slip into the long, off-the-shoulder dress that Maggie had designed, one in a different color for each of her attendants. Rebecca's was a pale sea-blue, which matched her eyes and set off her complexion. She brushed her hair until it lay in a rippling mass about her shoulders and placed a band of wild flowers around her forehead.

"Becca. . . ." There was a knock at her door. "Becca, are you in there?" It was Maggie.

"Yes! Come in."

"The men have already gone down to the pasture. All the chairs are filled and there are still more people arriving." Maggie swept breathlessly into the room, looking as pretty as Rebecca had ever seen her, in a cream-colored gown and a coronet of white blossoms. "Adam says we should start down as soon as we hear the fiddle. . . ."

"You look terrific," Rebecca said.

"I do?" The voice wavered but the bride seemed pleased enough.

"Yes, except for one thing. . . ."

"What's that?

"You're still wearing your tennis shoes."

Just as Maggie located the proper pair of slippers and put them on, they heard the vibrant piercing sound of the fiddle ringing out over the meadow. The four bridesmaids picked up their skirts and trailed down the tree-lined path that led from the house to the south pasture. In their pink, yellow, green and blue, they looked like a flock of butterflies on a late summer afternoon. Maggie followed close behind, holding on to Noel's arm.

The bearded lumberjack of a pianist saw them arrive and broke into the wedding march. Rebecca waited her turn, then caught her breath and moved slowly down the grassy aisle—step together step, step together step. The meadow was overflowing with people, occupying every available seat and perch and standing in a wide arc around the sides. And at the altar was Adam, fresh-scrubbed and handsome and grinning from ear to ear.

What a happy day, she thought as she watched the couple exchanging their vows. How much love in the air. A chorus of birds sang overhead in a deafening twitter as if determined to outdo both the pianist and fiddler. In the second row, she caught a glimpse of all four Mathesons, come to share in the celebration. "For better or worse," said Maggie. "Till death do us part."

So many things had finally come right for so many people. For Adam, the loner. For Maggie, buried in her work year after year. For Chris. For Mia. For Nancy and Ben Matheson. Her heart went out to them all. She sensed the fullness of their joy.

Then, all of a sudden, by contrast, the empty space inside her seemed emptier than ever. In the midst of the festivities, she was freshly aware of her own loss. She remembered a pair of dark eyes. A voice. A half-moon scar. The touch of a hand on her cheek. A swarm of images rose up and stung her from within.

"To have and to hold," Adam was saying. "To love and to cherish."

The oaths. These were the oaths that Nick Corelli wanted nothing to do with. He loved other things. His freedom. His art. The opening of the next show. Things other than her. She closed her eyes and took a deep breath.

The rich dark smell of the Mendocino earth assailed her senses, reminding her of what it was like to be close to him. No matter how much time and distance might lie between them, she was joined to him at the heart. Irrevocably. Forever. *I love you,* she thought silently. *Wherever you are, know that I love you.*

When she opened her eyes again, she could scarcely believe what she saw. She was so startled that she had to cover her mouth with her hand to keep from crying out. At first, she thought she had conjured up Nick's memory with such intensity that he only seemed to materialize before her. But a second glance revealed him to be flesh and blood. Standing with a group of latecomers, only a hundred yards away, he caught her eye and winked.

Rebecca was nonplussed. She realized belatedly that she must have made some kind of sound, because one of her fellow bridesmaids was shushing her from behind. The ceremony was coming to a close.

"I pronounce you husband and wife," said the minister. "You may kiss the bride."

It was Nick all right. She couldn't take her eyes off his face. She smiled wobbly. He blew her a kiss from the tips of his fingers. It was really and truly him. He had shaved off the beard and he looked a little different, but it was him.

A cheer went up from the congregation. The piano and the fiddle and the old Irish setter burst into triumphant song. Maggie and Adam swept up the aisle as husband and wife, and then, all at once, the nearly four hundred guests rose to their feet and dissolved into noisy joyful confusion.

Rebecca stepped down from the platform and started to make her way toward Nick, but an intervening wall of bodies blocked her path. She glimpsed him for a moment and then lost sight of him once more. "Bec-

ca!'' Chris and Mia Matheson were at her elbow.
"What a terrific wedding! Didn't Maggie look
great?''

"Yes...yes," she murmured absently. "Just
great...."

"Where are they going on their honeymoon?" Mia
asked brightly.

"I don't know. They won't tell. Excuse me for a
minute. I'll see you folks later, okay?" She had just
relocated Nick, stalled in conversation with Noel and
Gabe.

"Before you run off—" Chris caught her hand
"—I've got some good news for you."

"What's that?" It was all she could do to remain
patient.

"The last kitten. Mia wants it."

"Wonderful. I'm so glad. It's yours," she sputtered, kissing Mia on the cheek before she slipped
away at last into the crowd.

The wedding guests covered the meadow like bees
around a hive, swarming, soaring, buzzing with excitement. The champagne had been uncorked and was
being freely dispensed. Rebecca rejected a proffered
glass and pushed on toward the spot where she had last
seen Nick. But when she got there, he was gone. "Becca, darling." Maggie reached out and pulled her into a
circle of friends. "Thank you, thank you for all your
help."

"Congratulations, Maggie." She paused for a moment to embrace her new sister-in-law.

"He's here," Maggie whispered in her ear. "Have
you seen him?''

"Yes," Rebecca replied, "but not to speak to."

"Well, go find him. Good luck." Maggie smiled,
radiant with her own happiness. "I swear to you I
didn't know he was coming. It was as much a surprise
to me as anyone else."

Rebecca squeezed her hand and moved away into
the crowd once more, but she could never seem to ad-

vance more than a few steps without running into someone who wanted to speak with her. Everyone, it seemed, was either a childhood friend or a distant relative or an acquaintance from Shakespeare Bay or had recently seen her performance in *Romeo and Juliet*. She was soon dizzy with trying to return their greetings and explain that she couldn't talk just then, that there was someone she had to see first. At the same time, a new thought had begun to dawn on her: she really didn't know why Nick had returned. She had just assumed, upon the blissful shock of seeing him there, that he had appeared in response to her own deep feelings. But perhaps that was not the case at all. Perhaps he was back in California on business. Or to attend Maggie's wedding. Or a combination of the two.

She stood still amid the swirling throng and looked around for him again but he was nowhere to be seen. Adam caught her in a bear hug, ruffling her hair and exclaiming that she was the best sister in the world and that he had never been happier. Then Noel was embracing her. Then the best man and each of the ushers in succession. She was passed from one to the other like a dancer in a Virginia reel. Her head spun. The party was a kaleidoscope of colors and faces.

And, suddenly, she was in Nick's arms. Forgetting everything else, she threw her arms around his neck and clung to him. He laughed and picked her up and whirled her around, but still she would not let him go. Pride be damned. She was making an utter fool of herself but she didn't care. It was enough just to hold him close once more.

His mouth met hers in a long kiss that spoke of all the days and weeks and months spent apart. They stood there, oblivious to the rest of the world, enfolded in each other's embrace, unable to move or speak for what seemed an eternity. He felt so good and so dear and so warm that she could not imagine any other life outside his arms.

Eventually, reality reasserted itself in a chorus of high-pitched giggles surrounding them on all sides. Rebecca looked down to see a bevy of small children grinning up at them with fascinated curious faces. The imps whispered back and forth to one another and giggled again, and one tiny girl spontaneously pelted Rebecca and Nick with a handful of rice she had apparently been saving for the bride.

"Just what we need—munchkins," Nick growled in her ear. "Come on, let's get out of here."

She took his hand and led him down a path that curved past the makeshift chapel deep into a grove of oak trees. One gracious specimen offered them shelter, privacy and a couch in the form of a massive low-lying branch that hung parallel to the ground. "This was my special place when I was a child," she said. "I used to come here to play and daydream and to hide from the rest of the world."

Nick looked around and nodded approvingly. "I'm honored. Thanks for admitting me." He sat down upon the branch, testing it as it creaked beneath his weight.

He looked so handsome with his soft smoldering eyes and his clean-shaven chin. It was a very nice chin indeed, as Maggie had promised. He took off his jacket and folded it over the limb of the tree. She watched him wonderingly. She had never expected to see him again, much less here in this ancient sanctuary. "Nick...."

"Yes?"

"Why did you come back?" She couldn't help asking.

He smiled. "Well, I *was* invited...."

"I know. I was there when Maggie—"

"Maggie invited me," he acknowledged. "And then, a couple of days later, I got this sweet, formal little note from a Ms Rebecca Yates, who I had formerly thought held a very low opinion of me. The note wished me good luck with the play I was directing, so on and so forth—all very proper, you understand. But, after reading it twenty or thirty times, I began to see between the lines and I realized that this, too, was an invitation.''

She flushed. He held out his hand to her and drew her down beside him.

"So," Nick continued, "when the play opened in Rome and I once again found myself out of a job, I stuffed both invitations into my pocket and caught the first plane to the States." He plucked a drooping daisy from the garland in her hair and stuck it into his buttonhole, before softly covering her hand with his once more. She looked up at him. The light in his eyes was dazzling. She lifted his hand and brushed her lips across the back and then pressed it against her cheek. Nick leaned over and gently kissed her temple.

"I'm so glad you're here," she whispered.

"So am I."

"When do you have to go?"

"Well," he said thoughtfully, "I was offered another job in Rome...."

"Yes?"

"But I decided to turn it down. I've worked nonstop for the past several years and I deserve a vacation. I thought it might be fun to travel up and down the Pacific coast—Washington, Oregon, Yosemite, Big Sur, lots of places I've never been. What do you think? Are you game?"

"Am I game?" she repeated blankly.

"Sure. Does the trip appeal to you? Or is there somewhere else you'd rather go on a honeymoon? I'm open to suggestion."

Rebecca's mouth fell open. Before she could recover herself, Nick pulled her to him and kissed her three or four times, wooing her, claiming her, beguiling her, until she rested breathless in his arms. "What makes you so sure," she asked in an uneven whisper, "that I'll marry you?"

"I'm not," he told her. "I'm praying. Believe me,

I'm doing my best.'' He smiled and kissed her again. "But from the way you look at this moment—" his eyes roamed over her flushed and luminous face "—I think I may have reason to hope.'' Then, all at once, his gaze grew serious. "I love you, Becca. I want you to be my wife. I can't imagine it any other way.''

"Neither can I,'' she sighed. "Oh, Nicky, I've been in love with you for so long. I'll marry you this afternoon if the minister hasn't gone home.''

"Nothing doing,'' he said firmly. "After what I saw today, I want a big lush wedding. I want to see you walk down the aisle in a long white gown and a veil. I want to claim you in front of God and everybody. And then I want to carry you off with me, alone, just the two of us.''

"All right,'' she agreed, "that's what we'll do. When? Name a date.''

He was silent for a moment, thinking furiously. Then a sudden cloud came over his face. "Oh no. . . .''

"What? What is it?''

"Hamlet," he reminded her. "I completely forgot. When do you go into rehearsals?''

"In a couple of days.'' She faltered. This consideration had totally escaped her in the rapture of the present moment.

"Well, then,'' he conceded. "I think we'd better get married immediately, after all.''

"No.'' She made a quick but irrevocable decision. "I'm not going to do it. I'll tell Noel this afternoon. I don't want to spend this time with anyone but you.''

"Becca, I couldn't ask you to give that up.''

"Oh, no?'' she said. "Try me. You gave up a job to be with me, didn't you? I can surely give up one to be with you. There'll be other plays. But this time will never come again. This time is ours. I can't wait any longer. Believe me, it's what I want.''

Nick smiled. She had never seen him look so soft or so vulnerable. He had opened his heart to her at last. "You're sure then?'' he asked.

"Nothing means more to me than you do."

He gathered her into his arms and held her close. "Becca..." he murmured. "It's taken me so long to come to you. I feel like I've been searching all my life. I don't know how to tell you...."

"You don't have to," she whispered. "I know." There were no words. He found her mouth and then there was only the deep eloquence of silence.

An epic novel of exotic rituals
and the lure of the Upper Amazon

THE
TAKERS
RIVER
OF GOLD

JERRY AND S.A. AHERN

THE TAKERS are the intrepid Josh Culhane and the seductive Mary Mulrooney. These two adventurers launch an incredible journey into the Brazilian rain forest. Far upriver, the jungle yields its deepest secret—the lost city of the Amazon warrior women!

THE TAKERS series is making publishing history. Awarded *The Romantic Times* first prize for High Adventure in 1984, the opening book in the series was hailed by *The Romantic Times* as "the next trend in romance writing and reading. Highly recommended!"

Jerry and S.A. Ahern have never been better!

TAK-3

Share the joys and sorrows of real-life love with
Harlequin American Romance!™·

GET THIS BOOK
FREE as your introduction to Harlequin American Romance — an exciting series of romance novels written especially for the American woman of today.

Mail to:
Harlequin Reader Service

In the U.S.
2504 West Southern Ave.
Tempe, AZ 85282

In Canada
P.O. Box 2800, Postal Station A
5170 Yonge St., Willowdale, Ont. M2N 6J3

YES! I want to be one of the first to discover **Harlequin American Romance.** Send me FREE and without obligation *Twice in a Lifetime*. If you do not hear from me after I have examined my FREE book, please send me the 4 new **Harlequin American Romances** each month as soon as they come off the presses. I understand that I will be billed only $2.25 for each book (total $9.00). There are no shipping or handling charges. There is no minimum number of books that I have to purchase. In fact, I may cancel this arrangement at any time. *Twice in a Lifetime* is mine to keep as a FREE gift, even if I do not buy any additional books.   154 BPA NAZJ

Name _____ (please print) _____

Address _____ Apt. no. _____

City _____ State/Prov. _____ Zip/Postal Code _____

Signature (If under 18, parent or guardian must sign.)

This offer is limited to one order per household and not valid to current Harlequin American Romance subscribers. We reserve the right to exercise discretion in granting membership. If price changes are necessary, you will be notified.

AMR-SUB-1R